Grin & Barrett

Yolanda —
I'm so glad you're a part of my team!
Thank you :)
Ruth

Grin & Barrett

by

Ruth J. Hartman

Turquoise Morning Press
Turquoise Morning, LLC
www.turquoisemorningpress.com

Turquoise Morning, LLC
P.O. Box 43958
Louisville, KY 40253-0958

Grin & Barrett
Copyright © 2011, Ruth J. Hartman
Trade Paperback ISBN: 9781937389321
Digital ISBN: 9781937389314

Editor, Ayla O'Donovan
Cover Art Design by Stella Price

Trade Paperback release, August 2011
Digital Release, August 2011

Turquoise Morning Press
www.turquoisemorningpress.com

Warning: All rights reserved. The unauthorized reproduction or distribution of this copyrighted work, in whole or part, in any form by any electronic, mechanical, or other means, is illegal and forbidden, without the written permission of the publisher, Turquoise Morning Press.

This is a work of fiction. Characters, settings, names, and occurrences are a product of the author's imagination and bear no resemblance to any actual person, living or dead, places or settings, and/or occurrences. Any incidences of resemblance are purely coincidental.

This edition is published by agreement with Turquoise Morning Press, a division of Turquoise Morning, LLC.

I'd like to thank my publisher, Kim Jacobs from Turquoise Morning Press, for always believing in me. And also, my editor Ayla O'Donovan for her dedication and diligence to make my manuscript the best it could be.

And to my husband Garry.
My best friend and biggest fan.

Grin & Barrett

Remmie Grin is a self-sufficient dentist who has her life right where she wants it.

That is, until handsome, flirty Dr. Victor Barrett moves in next door. He constantly bugs her about selling her practice to him—but she's not budging.

How can she convince him to leave her alone when all she really wants him to do is kiss her again?

Chapter One

Grabbing the sides of the wooden stepladder, Remmie Grin squinted against the bright sunlight. The sign she'd hung in her front window tilted, just a little. Rats. She'd have to climb back up there to straighten it. Did the *New Patients Welcome* sound too pathetic? Did that sound as desperate as she felt? She'd like to kick the new dentist who was moving in right next door. Hard.

How obnoxious could he be? With all the empty buildings in town, why did Dr. What's-his-name have to come breathing down her neck? It made her want to spit. She wrinkled her nose. She'd worked her fanny off building her practice. Now she'd have to compete with the new guy. She wanted to claw at his ugly face.

This new dentist wouldn't know what hit him. When she was through with him, he'd be nothing more than a pile of dirt on the sidewalk. And as for the man's lawyers, she'd like to take a hunk out of their hide, too. Did they really think that calling her every single day would change her mind about selling her practice to them? Since they'd never revealed the name of the dentist, she'd have to come up with a name on her own. Hmmm. Gargoyle? Tarantula? Nah. Those names were too pretty for someone as repugnant as him. The creep.

"Looks good."

A deep velvety voice shot tingles down her spine. She turned and stared. A Greek god with ice blue eyes and salt and pepper hair stared back. Oh my. Would he object if she reached up and tousled that perfect hair? Her gaze traveled down to his massive shoulders. The fabric of his sports shirt straining over hard muscles. He must be a stranger in town because she'd never laid eyes on anyone as pretty as him.

"Thanks." Her breathing became shallow.

"So, you're taking new patients?"

"Yep." She crossed her arms. "Why, are you looking for a dentist?" What she wouldn't give to have him in her dental chair right now. His luscious lips close enough for her to lean down and....

"Not really."

"Oh." Drat. She had such dreamy plans for him.

"Just admiring the scenery."

He turned away from her and headed down the block.

No! She didn't want him to leave. "Wait, the scenery?" She frowned. It took four seconds for it to sink in that he'd meant her. Yikes. And he'd just walked away? How was that fair? It wasn't as if she got compliments from handsome men every day of the week. Not even the occasional Tuesday.

She blew out a frustrated breath as she picked up the lightweight stepladder, lugging it back inside her office. She leaned it against her front counter and snapped her hand back. She looked at her palm. A splinter, of course. Picking at the tiny wound only irritated her skin more. Hmmm. Too bad the handsome stranger from the sidewalk hadn't stayed. She'd gladly let him get out her splinter. Which would involve him holding her hand. Kissing her neck, her face, and her lips. She sighed. But he hadn't. So, she needed to put on her fuchsia big girl panties and get to work.

The town she lived in was small, so maybe she'd run into him again some time. At the very least, her postal carrier, June, knew everything about everyone. Maybe she would have a clue who the stranger was. If Remmie knew June, she'd have the stranger's coffee preference, shoe size, and contents of his glove compartment in no time.

Remmie carried the ladder through her patient waiting room, putting it to bed in her break room closet. There was always something besides dentistry to do around here. Painting. Repairing equipment. She needed a man. They were good at those things. But who was she kidding? If sidewalk man walked in her door right now, she had yummier ideas for him than fixing loose floorboards. She smiled, imagining running her hands over those big shoulders. Would they feel like granite? She'd love to be held by those rock-hard arms.

She grabbed her backpack from the Formica table. After changing into pale yellow scrubs, she was ready to prepare for her first patient of the day. But between dragging that blasted splintery ladder around, and drooling over the pretty man, she already felt like she'd worked a half a day. Instead, now she got to suction up someone else's drool. Well, yeehaw. She headed out to the waiting area.

"So, how does it look?"

Remmie glanced up to see her assistant and best friend Carla sitting at the front counter. "How did what look?"

"The sign?" Carla pointed behind her. "Isn't that what you were doing out there?"

"Oh. Right." Remmie walked to the counter.

"Why is your face turning red, Rem?"

"I-it's not." She put her hands to her cheeks. Would rubbing her face erase the red she was sure accompanied the heat? Darn her pale skin. It showed up too well next to her short dark hair; she never could hide how she felt. About anything.

"You look like a lobster that's been invited for dinner. As the main course."

"Um…I…." Shoot. Carla would make a huge deal out of this. Remmie adored her friend, but she could be nosy. And bossy. Maybe for Christmas she could buy her a special gift. Like a muzzle.

"Out with it Rem. You know you're going to tell me by the end of the day anyway. You might as well get it over with before Mrs. Kerris shows up for her appointment. But if I have to ask again in front of her, you know I'll do it."

Remmie shuddered. She knew Carla would indeed ask. And Mrs. Kerris was a blab. Thanks to the older woman now having a computer, e-mail made it possible to broadcast Remmie's secrets to the whole town in one quick click of her mouse. Why couldn't her nerdy son have given his mom something non-threatening? Like a blender. Then she could stir up chocolate milkshakes instead of trouble. "Well…."

"Go on." Carla's hands were on her red scrub-covered hips.

"I was hanging up the sign and there was this man…." *Please don't ask for details.*

"A man? Really? This is interesting. Keep talking."

Bother. Okay. "There's not much to tell. He noticed the sign, said he was admiring the scenery and walked off. He'd already left by the time I realized the scenery was…" Remmie twisted her hands together.

"What?"

Remmie swallowed hard. "Me." Her saliva must have taken a siesta. Because it sure was MIA from her mouth. Maybe if her dry tongue stuck to her palate, she could get out of saying more to Carla.

Carla raised her blonde eyebrows. "Now this is getting extremely interesting."

Remmie waved her hand dismissively in Carla's direction. "I don't even know his name."

"You don't think it could have been that new dentist in town, do you?"

"No. Tim down at the drug store described him as being sixty, short and bald. That didn't describe this man at all." Not even a little. If sidewalk man looked like that, Remmie's fingers wouldn't itch to grab his face and kiss him.

Carla bent forward. "Was this guy cute?"

"Well, yeah." Holy smokes, yes.

"There you go."

"There I go, what?" Remmie frowned.

"Rem, you've been treading water in a stagnant dating pool for some time now."

"Gee, thanks. Sounds smelly." She narrowed her eyes. If she growled at her assistant, would that scare her into letting this go? "Say, isn't it time for your yearly job review? I may have to change your pay. And I don't mean a raise."

"Ha-ha. Quit changing the subject."

Remmie sighed. She should have known Carla wouldn't let it drop. She was like a cat with tuna. Back off and keep your paws to yourself. "You're right. It has been a long time. Okay, an extremely long time since I had a date with someone who wasn't...."

"Atrocious?"

Remmie squinted at Carla. "Well, there is that. I was going to say obtuse, but they can go together, can't they?"

"Yep. Either way, you need a man."

She planted her petite hands on her hips. "Now look here. I wouldn't say I *need* a man. After all, I'm a successful dentist with my own business. And even though that business is small, I'm holding my own. I have a fairly good patient base, with loyal patients who usually are pleased with my work. So, I don't have to have a man." Remmie smirked. Carla knew her all too well. Well enough to know those were just excuses.

Carla winked at her.

Remmie grinned. "But yeah. It would be nice." Icy blue eyes. Perfect white teeth. Yes. Nice indeed.

****

After Remmie finished up her six morning patients, she plopped down at the front desk to finish filling out charts. It was a never-ending job—pure drudgery. But they had to be accurate down to the last comma. Too bad an office elf couldn't do it for her. She'd pay him. If she could find him. And if OSHA or HIPPA ever came calling, she wanted to be prepared with more than a 'gee, I don't know how that could have happened.' For some reason, government officials never found that amusing. The bell on the front door jangled. Usually Carla handled the front area, but she had stepped out to run a quick errand over lunch. Remmie didn't look up at the person at first. They could wait. She kept jotting down her notes, knowing if she stopped, she'd lose her train of thought. "I'll be right with you."

"No hurry."

The deep voice jarred Remmie's brain to attention. Shivers ran from her fingertips up to her collarbone. That incredible voice. She'd heard it before. Very recently. Her head snapped up and she locked eyes with the *scenery man* from that morning. How had he gotten even better looking since this morning? She'd swear his eyes were bluer. His muscled chest wider. Fumbling to set her charts aside, she popped up, trying to smooth the wrinkles from her scrubs. Who cared about OSHA when she could talk to *him*?

"Hello again. What can I do for you, Mr.....?" Sweet cakes? Honey bun?

"Just call me Victor."

"All right, Victor." She raised an eyebrow. Victor? She like Honey bun better. "How can I help you?" *Let me count the ways....*

Victor stepped closer to the counter. "I'm so sorry I didn't introduce myself this morning. I was in kind of a hurry, I'm afraid. I came to apologize. That was very rude of me."

"Oh, no problem. It's nice to meet you. I'm Remmie Grin." Why were her palms sweaty? She wasn't in seventh grade for Heaven's sake.

"Well, isn't that an unusual last name for a dentist? But then, I'm sure you hear that all the time." He stepped forward towards the other side of the counter. Because of his height, he had to bend down to place his elbows on it.

"You have no idea. If I didn't have a good sense of humor, it would really get on my nerves. I've even had a few people say they were sure I became a dentist *because* of my last name. Ridiculous, I know. Who in their right mind would go through eight years of college because of their name?" Why was she blathering on about her name? He probably thought she was an idiot. She breathed in his enticing aftershave, causing her to feel woozy. Now might be a good time for one of those old fashioned fainting couches. Those women knew what they were doing.

"Right. Some people have no idea what others go through."

"You've got that right." She watched his long fingers, mesmerized, as they tapped a quick beat on the countertop.

"The other reason I came in, besides to apologize, was to see if you could, maybe…"

Her head snapped up. His gorgeous blue eyes holding hers hostage. "Maybe what?" *Kiss you? Hug you? I can think of lots of things!*

"I'm new in town, you see, and I, well, I wondered if I could impose on you to answer some questions, possibly show me around a little bit? I'm sure with you being a dentist and all, you know quite a lot about the area."

Bells went off in Remmie's head. *He* wanted to spend time with *her*? *Yeehaw*. That would show Carla a thing or two about stagnant dating pools. She was ready for a swim in the ocean. "I'd be delighted, Victor."

"Splendid. May I call you Remmie?"

"Yes, of course." *Call me anything you want, Cutie-pie.*

"Wonderful. How about tonight, for dinner? Maybe you could answer some questions I have about the town, its people?"

"Sounds great." Yikes! He'd asked her out. What on earth would she wear? And what did her make-up look like at that moment? Was it sliding off her face as usual? Darn her tendency to sweat while she worked. She knew her scrubs were wrinkled. And her hair? Forget it. It often looked like that of a frightened chicken by lunchtime.

He checked his watch. "I'll pick you up here at, say, seven?"

"Perfect." She kept a smile on her face, but had to fight to control her breathing. Her stomach bounced and curdled. *Relax, Remmie. If you throw up on him now, he might rescind the offer.*

Victor opened the door to leave the office as Carla was coming back in. Her eyes bulged as she watched him head down the sidewalk. She started to close the door, then leaned back out for another long look.

"Remmie, who was that?"

"The man from this morning." And oh, what a man. Remmie fanned her face with her hand.

"Scenery guy?"

Remmie took a deep breath. "You got it."

"And...?" Carla raised her eyebrows.

"We're having dinner tonight." Did she just say that out loud?

Carla's mouth fell open.

"Close your mouth, Car, or fruit flies will move in."

"I just, he's just—"

Remmie leaned on the top of the counter with her chin in her hand. "I know. He really is."

****

Her afternoon was a mess. It wasn't cooperating very well. Or at least her patients weren't. Why did she have eight little rugrats scheduled all at once? The noise of shrieking kids was deafening. She'd have to remind Carla not to do that to her. She adored kids, but seeing that many in a row was a little much. And what was the school feeding them for lunch? Chocolate bars? Energy drinks? They were so hyper. One kid looked like he was on the verge of taking flight. She should have locked the break room door. Wouldn't want the little beast getting hold of her ladder for take-off practice. Besides, with her date that evening, it wasn't the best time to fall behind in her schedule while she tried to corral the little dumplings. She'd also have to remind parents not to drop their kids off in the waiting room and leave. Why would any parent do that? Did they think she ran a dental daycare? *No thanks, people. You gave birth to them. You make them behave.*

Two little girls cried during their cleanings. Which was strange considering they'd both had cleanings every six months for several years. Remmie had gritted her teeth, nearly popping off one of her crowns. One boy wanted to touch everything in sight, including Remmie's chest. Excuse me! Little Mr. Heffner needed some talking to. But the banner moment was when another little girl threw up the fluoride Remmie had just applied to her teeth. Yummy. Gotta love *that* smell. Thankfully, it didn't land on Remmie. But still so much fun to clean up. Ah, the joys of pediatric dentistry. *Clean up on aisle two.*

Finally at 5:30, she, Carla, and their part-time assistant Darcy, had everything straightened up, glued back together, and cleaned in the aftermath of kids-gone-wild. The permanent marker drawings on the waiting room wall would have to be painted over. With several coats. And that would have to wait. Not only didn't she have time to deal with it, she didn't have spare cash just floating around her office. They never did get a straight answer from the miniature Michelangelos as to where they got those markers or exactly who had done the deed. How many agencies would get involved if she tied the darlings to their chairs and muzzled their mouths? Might be worth it.

Remmie closed up the office and sped her car home to her old, two-story brick house. She needed a hot shower and tons of body wash. And she didn't even want to know what some of that slime in her hair was. Ick. As she soaped and rinsed, then massaged strawberry shampoo through her short hair, she got the wiggles. Her whole body was one big nervous tic. Should she consider it a date? Or just one of those, nice-to-meet-you kind of things? Either way, she couldn't go looking like she did right then. Uh-uh. No way. Rummaging through her closet for the seventh time didn't seem to produce anything different than the first six runs-through. Funny how that happened. But a girl could hope something fun and flattering appeared out of nowhere, couldn't she? Where were the closet elves when she needed them? Stupid, selfish elves.

Why did she wait until this moment to realize most of her clothes were outdated? Maybe because she wore scrubs to work and jeans the rest of the time. Or maybe because she usually didn't worry about what she looked like. She pulled black dress pants and a thin, peach-colored long-sleeved sweater out of her closet. Gold dangly earrings and a simple gold chain would complete the ensemble. It would have to do. At any rate, she'd look better than she had when he'd seen her earlier. But then, a party hat, fake beard and clown shoes would have looked better than that.

A squeaky sneeze caught her attention. She looked down to find one of her two cats sitting beside her. "Bless you, Charles." The solid gray shorthaired cat gazed up at her adoringly. His green eyes wide and unblinking. "I love you too, Charles, but I can't hold you right now. This is one time when I don't want to be covered in cat hair. Not that there's anything wrong with that. I just need to make a very good impression on Victor tonight."

A clunk from under her bed had her turning in the opposite direction. "Well, did you decide to join us, Winston?" The black and white tuxedo cat eased out from under the bed. He stretched his front legs, then his back ones, flicking his tail. He looked at Remmie and yawned. "I'm sure you were listening to my conversation with Charles, but in case you weren't, please refrain from rubbing against me. It's been so long since I had a date with someone who wasn't a troll; I don't want to take any chances by possibly offending him. You know how we hate trolls."

Even though she'd asked the cats nicely not to rub against her, she still found herself hopping out of their vicinity every time they leaned in her direction. She felt as if she were doing a river dance. "Come on, guys. Work with me, will ya?"

She foiled their advances by whisking her clothes back into the bathroom with her. She shoved the door extra hard to make sure it latched. Otherwise, they'd be right in there with her, sniffing and pawing, rubbing on her outfit. And if she'd left the clothes on her bed, they'd be kitty lounge pillows in a matter of seconds. Ah that'd be the life, wouldn't it? Lounge around on someone else's clean clothes all day. They'd feed you, pet you. No wonder her cats always purred. She'd purr too if someone did that for her. Victor? She had a feeling he could make her purr any old time.

She tackled her hair and makeup. She hardly ever took much care with either one, breezing through the task. When she worked, whatever she'd done with hair and makeup didn't last long anyway. Taking her mask and safety glasses on and off all day, didn't do much for either one. There were days she was surprised patients didn't scream, frightened by her scary appearance. But she took a few extra minutes this time. She glanced at the clock. Shoot! She'd have to rush to be back at her office by seven. What if he didn't wait for her? What if he was the kind of guy who got mad when you were late? Opening her bathroom door and leaping over her curious cats, she rushed down her stairs, grabbed her purse, and bolted out the front door.

Chapter Two

The clicking of high heels on cement caught Victor Barrett's attention. His lips curved into a smile as he watched Remmie rush down the sidewalk toward him. He sighed. She really was attractive. Maybe after she sold him her practice, she'd stay on and work for him. He wouldn't get tired of seeing that pretty face every day.

"So sorry I'm late," she said. "I had to park three blocks away. It seems as hard as I try, I'm always rushing everywhere."

"No problem. You were certainly worth waiting for."

Remmie blushed and smiled. "Why, thank you. That's so sweet."

He gazed down at her and smiled as he lightly placed his hand on the back of her elbow. Watching Remmie standing on her ladder that morning had given Victor a jolt. He'd been blindsided, not expecting the full figure. The short brown hair, just long enough to twist and play with. And those eyes. Those big brown eyes with long lashes made him think of bedroom eyes. He didn't even mind that she was short. All the more challenging to bend over, pull her tight against him, and plant a juicy kiss on those perfect pink lips.

Since she'd accepted his offer for dinner, he assumed she didn't have a husband, fiancé or boyfriend. She wasn't wearing a ring, at least. That should make his work easier. Just a little flirting should be all it took to get her to sell her practice to him. Uncle Tobias would be thrilled. He'd even bet he'd have the deal settled before the week was over. But, he'd have to remind himself this wasn't just a date. Victor wished he didn't have to bug her about selling her practice to him. But he wasn't given a choice. He had a job to do.

****

The restaurant, Fond Memories, was one of the finest in town. The times Remmie had been there were special occasions. When she got her braces off. Her 18th birthday. Her graduation from Dental School. She gasped when they pulled up in front of the door. She'd been trying to talk herself out of the fact that this was a date. She didn't want to get her hopes up. But, it had to be a date, didn't it? People didn't come here for run of the mill, how's-your-uncle kind of reasons. They walked inside. Something smelled heavenly. And it was crowded. How was Victor able to score a table on such short notice? He wasn't from here, so he wouldn't know anyone. Maybe a huge tip to the maître d'?

Victor pulled out her chair for her and waited until she was seated. How sweet. It was all she could do to keep her hands still in her lap. Her whole body fidgeted. Like cats high on catnip. She couldn't stop wiggling. When was the last time a man had held her chair for her? Not counting the little boy that afternoon who tried to whisk her operator chair out from under her before she could take a seat. She'd made sure he had to keep the fluoride tray with the bubblegum gel in his mouth for an extra minute, just to remind him who was in charge. The little ankle biter.

Remmie jumped when the waiter appeared at their table. She hadn't noticed him walk up. Being sneaky must be a prerequisite to working there. Maybe he wore soft tennis shoes? She leaned down a little to look. Nope. Just boring old black dress shoes.

He handed Victor a menu. She, however, did not receive one. What was up with that? Did the man not see her sitting there? She knew she was short, but good grief. *I'm hungry, too, Mr. Man.*

"Do you mind if I order for both of us?" asked Victor.

"Um...sure." She'd always seen that happen in movies, but had never been asked herself. She didn't think that ever really happened. Usually it made more sense to order for herself, although to be fair, most of her more recent dates took place at fast food places. There weren't waiters to serve you at French Fry Kingdom. She didn't want to appear rude by saying no. What if this was some weird new upper scale restaurant rule? But what if he ordered something she despised? She couldn't abide munching on something repulsive like octopus toenail cuticles. Even if it was smothered in ketchup.

Victor perused the menu and handed it back to the waiter. "We'll have the sirloin tips, rare, baked squash, and Caesar salad." He smiled at Remmie.

She smiled back, but squelched her inner ick. She didn't like anything he'd ordered for her. She was a well-done burger and fries kind of girl. But, considering the stagnant dating pool, and the length of time she'd spent treading water there, she held her tongue. She'd force herself to eat at least some of the repugnant fair.

"So Remmie, tell me about your dental practice." He fixed his blue eyes on hers.

Remmie blinked. Would someone not involved in dentistry want to hear what she did all day? Why would they? Most people didn't like going to the dentist, much less hearing the gory, saliva-related details. She'd almost gotten kicked out of a party once, when she supplied one too many details of a full mouth extraction. But hey, he asked. She'd give it a whirl. Maybe without the gore.

"That's so nice of you to ask, Victor." She smiled. "My practice is fairly new. I've only been out of dental school for seven years. I see both adults and children. And I do all procedures including root canals and extractions. I started out slow. Spending many of those first days staring at the office phone, begging it to ring. I'm happy to say now, though, that my schedule keeps steady, if not busy, all the time. My patients are the greatest. They make this job fun for me, even on very stressful days."

"Hmmm. Sounds wonderful. I'm sure your patients think a lot of you, too."

"I hope so." Except when she whipped out that needle.

"So, how many patients do you usually see in a day?"

"Um…I see anywhere from ten to fifteen, depending on what procedures I'm doing." She tilted her head. "Wow, you're really interested in what I do." Had she finally found someone she could discuss work with who wouldn't pass out?

Victor shrugged. "My uncle is a dentist."

"Ah, so you know something about dentistry then." Remmie picked up her glass.

"A little."

Remmie sipped her water. Over the rim of her glass, she watched him. His light blue tie matched his eyes, and the dove gray suit complemented his graying hair. Remmie always admired men who didn't color their hair. They looked distinguished and handsome with it natural. Women weren't always that lucky. Some women had gorgeous silver hair. Remmie wouldn't mind that. But in her extended family, the females were better off making a good friend out of their hairdresser. *Can you work me in today, please? My hair is the color of a possum's fur.*

When their meals were delivered, Remmie stared at it. Darn. As hard as she tried to change what was on her plate, it was still the same thing Victor had ordered for her. She had no desire to even taste any of it even though she was famished, but noticed Victor was watching her expectantly. She sighed and wrangled a microscopic piece of squash with her fork. Slowly, hoping Victor would get bored from watching her and turn away, she raised the vegetable to her lips. No such luck. He continued to watch her until it disappeared into her mouth. Only then did he begin on his own food.

"How do you like it, Remmie?"

She forced a smile when her first reaction was to grimace. "It's good. Really, really good."

"Wonderful. I knew you'd like it."

Well, Victor, you'd be wrong. She managed to eat as little as possible, hoping he wouldn't notice. At this rate, she'd have to stop for a pizza on the way home. They talked about the town, its people, its businesses and unique qualities. Remmie gave him the rundown from the bowling alley to the Baptist church. The more Remmie talked, the more she relaxed. Her hands no longer fidgeted. There was the occasional finger ripple, but that was all. This man seemed extremely interested in her town. She felt like a tourism bureau representative. *And to your right, Bald Jimmy's Hair Salon.*

Remmie couldn't believe how much they seemed to have in common. Although, when she thought about it, she did seem to be doing most of the talking. He mainly asked questions. Had he really said all that much about himself? Something was off here. People who kept quiet about themselves often had something to hide.

Remmie picked up a roll and buttered it. At least that was something tasty. Who didn't like a big hunk of bread and a glob of actual butter? Should be safe enough. She eyed Victor over the top of the bread. Now it was time to find out more about her dinner companion. "So, Victor, you now know all about me, but you never told me what it is you do for a living."

"I didn't? Oh. Sales."

"Oh, okay. What do you sell?"

He shrugged. "Oh, this and that." He poured himself a second cup of coffee from the carafe on their table.

She raised her eyebrows. "This and that. Hmmm. Sounds intriguing." Okay, so his job was boring.

"Trust me. It's not that exciting. I'd rather talk about you."

He leaned toward her, placing one forearm on the edge of the table. His gold cufflink shimmered. He smiled, showing gleaming white teeth that Remmie could tell were expensive crowns. His blue eyes sparkled from the candlelight at a nearby table. She could look at him all night and not get bored.

At first Remmie was flattered. When was the last time a man was actually interested in her? But something was off here. Why was he being so evasive about what he did? Most men liked to talk about themselves. A lot. Some even so much that she wanted to run away screaming. That was one advantage to being a dentist. If they started talking too much while in her dental chair, she could always shove a saliva ejector in their mouth.

Was Victor a mobster, a hit man or IRS? Or even worse, married? And wait, he'd never even told her his last name, had he? *Think, Remmie.* She had told him hers when they were in her office. Or had she been so excited to be on a real date, she'd missed some of what he'd said. And at this point it seemed rude to ask. She couldn't say, 'Excuse me, Mr. uh, whatever, who are you again?'

"Well, look who's here, Dean."

Remmie looked up to see June, her postal carrier, standing beside her husband. "Hi June. Hi Dean. Nice to see you." Perfect. Just when she needed to find out more about Victor.

June grabbed Dean's large, meaty hand. "It's our twentieth wedding anniversary. Otherwise, our dining experience tonight would be the Burger Barn."

Remmie laughed. "I hear ya. Congratulations, you two." She tilted her head in her date's direction. "This is Victor."

June glanced at Remmie's dinner companion and did a double take. "It *is* you. I told Dean it was you. He didn't believe me."

Remmie looked at Victor. He twisted in his seat. Why was he fidgety? Had he had some catnip, too? "You two know each other?" She thought Victor was new in town. How could she have missed meeting him before now?

Ignoring Remmie's question, Victor addressed June. "Hello," he said, "nice to see you. Congratulations on your anniversary."

June smiled at Remmie. "Isn't this fun? Two dentists out on the town together. You'd think it was a dental convention or something. Gosh, and you're neighbors, too. I found that out on my mail delivery route." She turned to her husband. "Remember, I told you Dr. Barrett's new office is right next to Remmie's."

Remmie's face heated up. So did her earlobes. That only happened when she was extremely steamed. She twisted the cloth napkin in her lap to a tight knot. Narrowing her eyes at Victor, she stared, but said nothing. She wanted to scratch those perfect white crowns off of his teeth and toss them in his salad for croutons. How dare he trick her like this?

A few more pleasantries about June's mail route were exchanged before June and Dean finally wandered toward the door. Remmie's first impulse was to kick him under the table. But she didn't. What if he kicked her back? *Yeah, but I'm wearing high heels, dude.*

Barely suppressing a growl, Remmie whispered, "And just when were you planning to tell me that, *Dr. Barrett?*"

He sighed. "To be honest, I was hoping you wouldn't find out for a while."

"Excuse me?" Had he really admitted that?

"I was trying to get on your good side. You need to sell me your practice."

"When pigs do the splits!" Her voice grew louder with each word.

"Well, that was certainly rude." His fork clattered on his plate.

"Me? You're calling me rude? You lied to me. I'd heard the dentist next door to me was older, short and bald. Besides, you got me to have dinner with you. I even thought it was a—"

"Date? It was. And the man you're describing is my uncle. It's not my fault you had bad information from someone else. But as for our date, weren't you having a nice time?" He wiped his mouth with his napkin.

"Yes, until I found out you just want to get your mitts on my practice." She still wanted to kick him. Hard.

"Okay. I'll admit I want to buy your practice, but I also wanted to go out with you. You're very attractive. Just my type, in fact."

Her earlobes were on fire now. "I don't think so. Your type would be more like…like Medusa."

Victor drummed his long fingers on the table. "Now you're being silly."

"Oh! You insufferable snake." She narrowed her eyes.

"I guess that goes along with your Medusa theory, at least."

"You're impossible. I wouldn't ever sell my practice. And especially not to you."

Victor looked around the restaurant. "Please, lower your voice. Everyone is staring."

"So what? They need to know what kind of fiend you are. If you're going to be hanging around town, they need to hide their pets and young children. Ogres like you can't be trusted."

"Fiend? Ogre? My goodness. You have quite the imagination. Not to mention an extensive vocabulary."

Remmie stood up, knocking over her chair in the process. She grabbed her fork and held it up. Would she get in trouble if she impaled him with it? Just a little? She shook her head. Nope. He wasn't worth it.

Victor's eyes widened. He stood up from his chair. "Tell me you weren't thinking of stabbing me with that thing."

The maitre d' came rushing to her side and righted the chair. "Miss, what seems to be the problem? Was your meal not satisfactory?"

She had hated the food, but it wasn't this man's fault. It was Victor's. And she'd allowed him to order for her, so the blame was hers, too. She was so angry she couldn't form the words to answer the waiter. She grabbed her purse and stomped out of the restaurant. She realized everyone in the place was staring at her, but she kept going. Once outside, she remembered she didn't have her own car. Wonderful. She'd have to hoof it. Throwing the strap of her brown leather purse over her shoulder, she held her head high, determined not to cry, yell, or spit.

Two blocks away from the restaurant, a loud crack of thunder boomed. Remmie looked up at the graying sky with a distrustful eye. Half a block later, the skies opened and dumped gallons of rain on her head. Splendid. Now it wouldn't matter if she cried. Or spit for that matter. Who would know since she was drenched? If the writer of "Singin' in the Rain" changed the first word to "Cussin'" they'd know her present mood.

A car slowed as it approached her. Even with rain dripping in her ears, Remmie could hear the purr of the expensive motor. She turned her head. Victor. Of course. The man was irritating and hard to shake. Like poison ivy.

"Remmie," he said through the rolled down window. "Get in, will you?"

"Forget it."

"You're getting soaked."

She glared at him. "What do you care?"

"Remmie, I'm sorry I made you mad. Will you please get in?"

She shook her head, spraying droplets of water on her already soggy sweater. "No. You're a snake."

"We've already established that you think I'm a reptile. So, be that as it may, please just get in."

Remmie hated to give in. Especially to someone like him. His pushiness and patronizing attitude reminded her of her father and brothers. She'd had enough of that to last a lifetime. They always made her feel as if she was sub-par. Not smart enough to make it on her own. Not tough enough to stick out eight years of school to be a dentist.

But she was cold. And wet. And the moisture was seeping into some very uncomfortable, private places. It would serve him right if her wet clothes ruined the expensive upholstery of his sports car. *Oh well, sorry you have to spend a gazillion dollars to have your car cleaned.*

She yanked open the door and plopped down into the seat. Her sodden peach sweater squished streams of water down the back of the seat, pooling around her hips. Water squirted out her shoes when she planted her feet in the lush beige carpet.

"A tad damp, are we?" He pulled the car away from the curb.

"Shove it."

"My, my, Remmie, you certainly have a temper."

Her eyes widened. "Who could blame me? You tricked me."

"Did I ever lie to you?"

"Not exactly. But you'd win the blue ribbon for evasiveness."

"It's not a crime, you know." He drummed his fingers on the steering wheel.

"But it's sneaky. And I don't like it."

"Okay, then, we've established that I'm a snake and evasive. Anything else?"

She pointed her index finger at him. "Don't get me started."

He grinned. "But you're cute as all get-out when you're mad."

"Oh you...you—"

"Don't call me a *you-you*."

She glanced at him to see if he was serious. His smirk looked like one of her cats when they deposited something slimy and unmentionable in her underwear drawer.

Her eyes widened. "Are you laughing at me?"

"No. Wouldn't dare. Let's get you home so you can get dried off."

She harrumphed and crossed her arms. Which caused more water-squishing. *Oh!* Victor snickered in the driver's seat, but Remmie refused to give him the satisfaction of looking at him. So she looked out the side window instead. She leaned her damp forehead on the cool glass. And steamed it up with her sigh.

"Remmie, what will people think?" His eyes darted to the window.

"Oh! I..."

He laughed.

"Of all the…inconsiderate, evil, troll-like things to say." She blew out an irritated breath.

"Troll-like?"

"Never mind. You had to be there." She turned her head away from him.

"Ah. And who were you talking to about trolls?"

"My ca— Never mind."

They drove the short distance to Remmie's car. There was no place for Victor to park nearby, so he headed to her office. Remmie wished he would have just let her out right there on the street. The less time spent with him the better. But the annoying man kept on driving. She thought about opening the door and jumping, but with her luck, she'd break both legs and her jaw.

He pulled in front of her office and turned off the engine. Before she could even undo her sodden seatbelt, he'd opened his door, trotted around the front of the car, and opened her door.

"I'll walk you to your car, Remmie."

"That's not necessary."

"Of course it is."

She sighed. "Stop pretending to be human, Dr. Barrett. We both know you're not."

"Oh. Right. A reptile."

She glanced at him. He was smirking. Again. She'd like to smack that smirk right off his lips. His full, kissable lips. Ah! What was she thinking?

Realizing she wouldn't get away from him until he walked her to her vehicle, she stomped the distance between it and his sports car. And squished the whole way. Gravity sucked the water dripping from her hair and clothes, trickling down her legs into her shoes. Key in hand before they reached it, she was ready to jump in her car and be away from him. Her plan was to grab a pizza, warm shower and be in her pajamas within the hour. Maybe by then she'd forget the impulse to poke the man in the eye. Repeatedly.

"Oh no, you don't, Dr. Grin."

He took her hand and freed the keys. Easily sliding the key into the lock, he opened the door. She scrambled around him, intent on getting her drippy self away from him and home as quickly as possible. She never wanted to talk to him again. It didn't quite work out that way.

She looked up at him and gasped. "Hey, what are you—"

"I love a challenge, Remmie. And you've given me one, playing hard to get." His lips on hers squelched the last word.

She fought the kiss. At first. But a wonderful drugged sensation took over her mind and body. Desire. Warmth. What was happening to her? She said bye-bye to common sense and indulged in the incredible kiss. His arms, muscular and long, wrapped around her waist and pulled her close. She had to stand on her tiptoes in her high heels to reach her arms around his now-wet neck. Drat the family short gene she'd inherited. She could taste the coffee he'd had during their meal. She'd never been fond of coffee before. But, tasting it on Victor's lips gave it a whole new flavor. Mixed with the rainwater on both their faces, it was perfect. If she could drink it this way, she'd have it every day. She'd been kissed a lot in her lifetime, but those guys had been amateurs compared to Victor. Where did the man learn to use his lips like that? Her fingers sifted through his hair, as she tried to get even closer to him. But, alas, he pulled away.

"There now. That wasn't so bad was it?"

She opened her eyes. And blinked. He was talking. Why was he talking? Way too much talking. Needed more kissing. She looked at him. Smirking. The cad was smirking. *Again.* Oh! She shoved her hands at his damp sport coat.

"Kindly let go of me, Dr. Barrett."

"You didn't seem to mind a couple of minutes ago. Besides, I'd like to do it again. You do something to me, Remmie."

"Well, I…but…just…oh! Let me go."

He laughed, further infuriating her.

She kicked him.

"Ouch!" Grabbing his shin, he hopped on the other leg.

Remmie grabbed the keys, jumped in her car, slammed the door, and revved the engine. Victor jumped out of the way of the front wheel right before losing his toe.

Remmie smiled. *Who's laughing now, Victor?*

Chapter Three

Carla's mouth hung open. "You did what?"

"I said, I kicked him."

"That man. The gorgeous one? You kicked him?"

"Carla, that man happens to be none other than Dr. Victor Barrett." Remmie crossed her arms.

Carla made the *so-what* shrug.

"From next door. You know, who wants to buy my practice?"

Carla shook her head, her blonde hair swishing against her cheek. "No way."

"Yes, way."

Carla sighed. "And here I thought he was the one who would save you from drowning in the stagnant dating pool."

"Yeah, well, you weren't the only one."

"So, Rem, did you kiss him?"

Remmie's face heated up.

Carla bobbed her head. "You did! You kissed him."

"Well, yeah."

"But if you don't like him, then…why?"

Remmie sighed. "Oh, Carla, you've seen him. I may be stupid, but I'm not dead."

Remmie wished the outcome of her date had been different. Oh, how she wished that. The kiss was…breathtaking. Literally. It was as if she'd forgotten how as Victor's lips claimed hers. But, to find out who he was. And what he was trying to do. He wanted her to sell out to him. No way was that going to happen. Great kissing or not. No tempting, seductive, sexy lips were worth that.

Noisy workmen were in Victor's office next door. Patients complained. Children were frightened. Babies cried. Carla rolled her eyes about it all day. Darcy kept asking how long they'd have to put up with it. And Remmie was on edge. Not only from the drilling, thumping and sawing, but also from her memories of kissing Victor. *That kiss.* Every time she tried to focus on her work, there it was again. How had she allowed that to happen in the first place? She'd just found out he was the moron who wanted to buy her out. And yet, she still kissed him? Traitorous, untrustworthy lips. She couldn't take them anywhere. May as well send them away to day camp.

Maybe she was destined to stay single. If Victor Barrett was the best candidate to ride down the dating path in years, then there wasn't much hope, was there? At least she had her practice. No matter how much he bugged her, he could never force her to sell. She'd have her work until she was old and withered. Ewww. That painted a pretty picture. Her, old and decrepit. Hobbling out to the waiting room to retrieve her patients. Taking five hours to do a procedure she did now in twenty minutes. And she doubted Carla would be there then. She'd most likely find someone, get married and have a family some day. Even if she kept on working for a while, who could blame her for not wanting to spend her whole life in this dental office? Just like Remmie seemed destined to do.

And she had her cats. Who she loved. They were her family. Yep. That would be her life. Work. Cats. No man. Was that enough?

****

Inside the grocery store, Remmie grabbed a cart. She rummaged in her large denim purse for her grocery list as she pushed her squeaky shopping cart with her other hand. Why did her purse always eat whatever it was she was looking for? Items migrated to the bottom, never to be heard from again. And it didn't seem to have any particular favorites, either. Keys, cell phone, pieces of paper and sugar-free gum all seemed to be on the menu.

She waved at one of her patients as she guided the cart towards the right side of the store. Checking out the new selection of romance books, she bent over to pick one up from the bottom shelf. Turning it over to read the blurb on the back, she sighed. Ah. Tall handsome doctor falls in love with his nurse when they're stranded on a desert island. Sounded too good to be true. But, with no man in her life, she may as well read about someone else's. She turned the book over to look at the beautiful couple embracing next to a waterfall on the cover. With her other hand, she pushed her cart forward.

"Would you kindly watch where you're going, Dr. Grin-who-kicked-my-shin?"

Remmie knew who it was before she even lifted her gaze. She wasn't in the habit of kicking people, so it had to be *him*. Of course he was here. Why should her shopping experience be exempt from Dr. Bugs-me-so? "Why hello, Dr. Barrett. How nice to *run into* you." With that, she pushed her cart into his, jostling the groceries he'd already purchased. The miniature earthquake effect jumbled his vegetables.

"Hey. You smashed my cumquats."

She snickered. "You should be very proud. Not every man can boast that." She placed the book in her cart and maneuvered around him as she scurried down the first aisle. Aware that some of the store's customers were watching the two dentists, she glided on down the aisle, acting as if it didn't bother her to be a centipede under their collective microscope. People in a small town were so nosy. Remmie had no doubt her argument with Victor at the restaurant was already being talked about by everyone. And that kiss. Right out on the street. Under a streetlight. She hoped someone didn't snap a picture with their cell phone. Or even worse, gotten a video. It might end up on YouTube! What had she been thinking? Oh, yeah. She'd let her lips do her brain's job for a while. Not smart.

Her journey down the second aisle left her and her cart unscathed. She tossed in boxes of crackers, cereal and bread. She debated over a bag of chocolate chip cookies. What the heck? They sailed into her cart as well. Chocolate bars? In they went. She was glad her young patients weren't witnessing this. She wasn't practicing what she preached. Everybody deserved at least one vice, in her opinion. She glanced in her cart. Better make that two vices.

The third aisle, however, caught her off guard. As soon as she rounded the end cap containing cans of low-sodium tomato soup, her cart was jolted. And so was she. Victor, sporting that smirk she despised, was hunched down behind the handlebar of his cart. His icy blue eyes peered at her over the metal bar. He looked like a deranged meerkat.

Remmie pushed her long bangs out of her eyes. "What are you doing ramming my cart? Were you lying-in-wait ready to pounce on me?"

Victor stood up to reach his full six-foot-two height. "Of course not. Wow, you really do have an active imagination. I just wanted to see that lovely face again. Only dry, this time." He took his cart and pushed around her, leaving barely a half-inch between their carts. As he strolled in the opposite direction, he used his fake smile on two ninety-something women. "Ladies. Nice to see you. Aren't you both looking beautiful? And I love your hats. Have a great day." The two women giggled and simpered like junior-highers.

Remmie gritted her teeth. Of all the nerve. How could one man be so charming to some people and so troll-like to her? And only to her? She hadn't seen him be outright rude to anyone else. What a creep. He was a wolf in dentist's clothing. And yet, she'd kissed those lupine lips. She was one weak woman. How was she going to avoid seeing him every day when he'd be working right next door?

Deciding to get her shopping done quickly so she could get away from him, she picked up her pace. Checking her list, which she'd finally found as she tromped down aisle two, the only things left were from the fresh produce section. *Ah, almost done. This shouldn't take long, then I can skeedattle outta here.* Stepping around the corner, she glanced both ways before heading toward the lettuce bin. Wonderful. No other dentists in sight.

"Isn't this cozy?" asked Victor. He leaned against the handle of his cart and smiled at her.

Perfect. "Where did you come from?"

"Oh, you poor thing. Is your memory going, too?"

"What do you mean, 'too'?" She glared at him.

"Well, you obviously have trouble having a nice date without committing violence. And your practice could use several dozen more patients, couldn't it?"

Trying to reign in her temper but realizing it was probably too late for that, Remmie decided to address his first insulting comment. "What did you mean about my memory?"

He reached down and rearranged his groceries in the cart as he spoke. "You asked where I came from. Did you already forget that we're neighbors?"

"Ha-ha. Gee, that's so funny I forgot to laugh."

"What does that mean, anyway? I've always wondered. Although I must admit, I haven't had anyone say that to me since I was...oh, I don't know...twelve?"

She tightened her grip on the handle of her grocery cart. "And just what was that crack about my dating life? And my practice? Both are going quite well, thank you very much."

"Is that so? Hmmm. My mistake, I guess. I assumed when you accepted my dinner invitation you weren't seeing anyone."

He reached into his cart rearrange his groceries. Again. Was he alphabetizing them?

"But," he said, "here's a question I've been meaning to ask ever since you had the enjoyment of meeting me."

She rolled her eyes, but couldn't resist asking. "What?"

"What is Remmie short for, anyway?"

Her hands balled up in fists. "Did you just call me *short?*"

In mock horror, he held up his hands in front of his face. "Please, please, Dr. Grin. Don't hit me. For that I'd have to get down on my knees so you could reach me."

"Oh, you're such a…" *Think…make it good, Remmie.* "You, you, meanie, you!" *Yeah, girlfriend, that ought to show him.*

Victor's laughter erupted in a snort as he wiped tears from his face. His whole body shook. "I'd sincerely like to thank you for the best laugh I've had in ages. Honestly, I really needed that. I was going to rent a comedy from the movie section over there, but now I won't have to. You saved me a couple of bucks."

Remmie could stand it no longer. She'd tried. She'd tried to hold in her temper. She'd tried to play nice. But how could a person play nice with an abhorrent jerk? He'd pushed her too far. Acting as if he liked her. Kissing her senseless. Then trying to pry her practice away from her. And now he was making fun of her? Enough was *enough.* The head of romaine lettuce she flung at Victor's head hit him square on his left sideburn.

"What the...?"

"Ha, take that, you creep." She dusted off her hands on the front of her jeans. She was halfway turned away from him when the tomato struck her in the cleavage. And left a horrid red stain behind. Small seeds and pulp clung to her formerly clean, white, v-neck t-shirt. She shivered as pieces of the cold, wet fruit slid down inside her bra. "Oh! How dare you. Look what you did." She plucked the slimy stained fabric away from her skin.

"Look what *you* did." He gingerly picked at fragments of a lettuce leaf that clung to his hair. "Do you have any idea how much I have to pay my personal barber to get my hair to look like this?"

"You actually pay someone to do that to you? I figured you stuck a bowl on your head and let a neighborhood rodent gnaw his way around the edges."

His mouth dropped open at that, and he sprinted to the watermelon bin.

Remmie narrowed her eyes. "You wouldn't dare."

"Wanna bet? Watch me, Shorty."

Remmie ducked just in time. The football-sized fruit sailed over her and splattered on the floor in front of the refrigerated orange juice. Fruit, juice and seeds congregated in a messy, pink pool.

Victor pointed toward the sticky mess. "Now look what you've done."

"Me?" she screeched. "How is that my fault?"

Victor raised his voice. "You threw the lettuce."

"You threw that tomato."

"You started it."

"Hey!" A loud male voiced stifled their argument. "I don't care who started it. But you're both going to pay for it." Remmie and Victor turned to see Mr. Hennings, the large, gruff no-nonsense store manager, standing behind them with his massive arms crossed. Remmie had heard the rumor that he'd been a semi-professional boxer in his youth. His frown couldn't mean anything good. "And if anything like this ever happens again, you will both be banned from the Piggly Wiggly. Got it?"

"Yes, Sir," Remmie and Victor said in unison. Was Victor feeling remorse about something? Remmie was. She wanted to die of embarrassment. The town would have something juicy to talk about now. Juicier than the pink glob on the floor. Now would be a wonderful moment for the sticky floor to swallow her up.

The store manager pointed a stubby finger toward the front of the store. "Take your purchases up front and check out before I change my mind and kick you out right now."

Remmie ducked her head and hurried behind her cart in that direction. Victor, not to be outdone even when they'd been chastised, raced ahead of her. He skidded to a stop at the only available checkout line. Karole, the checkout girl, stared at him. Her mouth was hanging open. It was apparent to Remmie, who stood behind Victor in line, that the entire store heard and saw what happened. How could they not? Up until now the most exciting thing to happen at the Piggly Wiggly was a free can of sauerkraut when you bought a package of pork sausage.

Victor leaned toward the girl. "Please go ahead and check me out, if you would. I need to get away from some of the riff-raff in this establishment." He gave her a flirty smile as he pointed behind him to Remmie.

Remmie thought she might lose her lunch, right then and there. *Oh, good grief.*

Victor paid for his groceries and left the store. Remmie placed her food on the conveyer belt. "Sorry about that, Karole. I'm mortified, and he doesn't make it any easier."

Karole leaned toward her. "What's with that guy anyway?"

Remmie sighed. "I wish I knew."

"You know, this kind of reminds me of my little brother."

Remmie raised her eyebrows. "Excuse me?" She must have *some* little brother.

Karole grabbed a package of cookies and scanned them. "You know how little boys are. When they like a girl, they act like they don't like her. Pull her pigtails and stuff. It doesn't make any sense, but that's how they act."

Remmie laughed. "Oh, no. I'm quite sure that's not the case at all. Believe me."

Karole smiled and shrugged. "You never know."

Remmie smiled back, but inwardly shivered. Ick. What an awful thought. The only thing she liked about Victor was his kiss. And she'd make sure that never happened again.

Her face still felt hot after she'd left the store and placed her sack of groceries in the back of her vehicle. Why did she let that man get to her? She'd never reacted this strongly toward a man before. Maybe once he got it through his gorgeous thick skull that she wasn't selling her practice to him, he'd leave her alone. And move to Tibet.

Slamming the trunk lid, she gasped. She glimpsed a shadow at her feet. Someone stood right behind her! She whipped around, ready to slug the daylights out of whoever the would-be cookie thief was. She was glad to be wearing her big, pointy garnet ring. That would give him a poke in the eye.

She looked up and sighed. "Oh. It's only you."

Victor frowned. "What do you mean *only*?"

"Why are you following me? Haven't you caused enough trouble today?"

Victor placed his hand over his chest. "You've wounded me, Remmie. Deeply."

"If I wasn't so mad at you, that might make me laugh."

"Why would you be mad? I'm the one with the ruined hair." His hand reached up to smooth a microscopic follicle indiscretion.

"Don't go there, mister. You ruined my shirt. There's not enough bleach in this hemisphere to remove those stains." She pointed towards her tee shirt. "And this was one of my favorite shirts."

"But what's a shirt compared to my hair? My *hair*."

Remmie blew out a breath. What was with this guy? "Look, Victor, this isn't a good time to get in another argument with me."

He cocked one eyebrow. "You're right. I'd rather do this."

He pulled her to his chest so fast she stumbled.

"Hey, what the—"

"I just can't seem to get enough of you, Remmie." His lips met hers, blocking out her reply.

Her hands, along with her purse and keys, were trapped between them. Why were his kisses so intoxicating? Her mind told her to back away. Now. Her lips, however, seemed to have taken control. Why were her stupid lips so weak when it came to this man? This annoying, bothersome, sexy, intoxicating man. She leaned against him. The more he kissed, the more she felt like melted butter. She was surprised her legs hadn't seeped into the pavement. Even the sharp poke of car keys in her tomatoey chest didn't faze her.

Victor ended the kiss, brushing his lips against hers one last time. He rubbed his thumb on her cheek. "Remmie, you've cast a spell over me."

Her ears perked up. Wait. What was that noise?

Clapping. *Clapping?*

She tried to pull away from Victor. But he wouldn't budge. His arms were like metal bars, holding her against his chest.

"But, honey, I'm not ready to let you go yet," he said.

Remmie looked around. Several people stood there. Clapping. *Oh no!*

"Way to go, Docs."

"Man, dentists sure are more exciting than I ever thought."

"Mommy, why is that man grabbing that lady's bottom like that?"

Remmie gasped. She looked down. Sure enough, that's where Victor's hand resided at the moment. The boy, no older than four, was one of her patients. Wonderful. His mom grabbed the boy's hand and tugged him away, giving Remmie an evil glare in the process.

Victor smiled at the crowd. "Okay people. Show's over. Go back about your business."

The small group dispersed, leaving Remmie alone again with Victor.

Remmie wriggled around until he let go of her. "Get off of me."

"But Remmie, you seemed willing a minute ago."

"That's because, well, because, I—"

Victor smiled. "Exactly."

"Oh, you—"

He held up his hand. "Please, if you call me a you-you again, I may have to repeat that kiss. Just to shut you up."

She smacked her fist containing her car keys against her thigh. "Oh!" And stomped around him to unlock her car.

Chapter Four

Remmie heard the bell on the front office door. Carla headed that way.

Here we go, thought Remmie. Should be an interesting day, at the very least.

Her 8:30 patient, Harold Ballentine, was ninety-eight years old. At least. Remmie knew it would take an extra fifteen minutes or so for the man to make his way from the reception area to one of the patient chairs. And it wasn't because he walked slow. Well, he did actually, but more because he liked to talk. A lot. She smiled. Mr. Ballentine was one of her favorite patients. She knew all his stories by heart. But they were all entertaining, at least.

Carla stood in the entrance way between the waiting room and the patient care area. "Good morning. We're ready for you Mr. Ballentine."

Remmie stood right behind her. She and Carla had a small bet on the exact number of minutes it took the man to make the journey. Whoever was closest got a chocolate bar.

The man gazed up at them from his seat. It would have been better if they'd never let him sit down out there in the first place. That added at least five minutes to their start time.

Mr. Ballentine wiggled his white caterpillar-resembling eyebrows. And they had wings. Maybe if they could fly, they'd get him to the patient chair faster. She could just picture something out of Peter Pan, her patient flitting around the room.

"Must be my lucky day," he said.

Remmie smiled. She knew what was coming. "Why's that?"

"Because I get to spend time with two beautiful ladies."

Carla smiled, too. "Well, isn't that a sweet thing to say?"

"Yep. I'm a lucky, lucky man."

He hadn't moved from his chair yet.

Carla tried again. "We're ready for you in the back, if you'd like to follow me." She pointed behind her.

He settled more firmly into the gray upholstered chair. "Did I ever tell you about the time I took a vacation to the Grand Canyon? I very nearly fell in that great big hole."

"Uh-oh," whispered. Remmie. "This is one of his longer stories."

Carla whispered back. "And that's saying something."

Remmie walked over to sit beside Mr. Ballentine. She waited until he took a second to breathe while immersed in his elongated tale.

"Mr. Ballentine. I'd really love to hear the rest of the story." *Even though I've heard it at least fifty-nine times.* "But we need to get started on you so you can get on with the rest of your day. Don't you usually meet some of your friends at the diner for lunch? Maybe you could tell me the rest of it while you're waiting to get numb. How would that be?" *Please say yes.*

The man squinted his eyes. "Yes, yes you're right. I *am* meeting my friends for lunch. Wouldn't want to get there too late and miss out on the senior 10:30 a.m. lunch special, now would I?"

His knees creaked and cracked as he eased into a half-sitting/half-standing position. Remmie stood up, ready to grab an arm if he started to fall. He wavered, rocking back and forth between standing mostly upright and slumping back to the chair. This part always made her nervous. What if he fell? She'd feel awful.

Remmie leaned closer to him. "Would you like some help? These chairs sit really low. Lots of people have trouble getting out of them."

"They do?"

"Sure do."

"She's right," said Carla. "Happens every day."

Mr. Ballentine barked a laugh. "Now you girls are pulling my old leg, aren't ya? Just trying to be nice to an old man."

Remmie linked her arm through his. "We like you, Mr. Ballentine. We're glad you're here."

He smiled. The Grand Canyon story apparently forgotten. "Yep, I'm a lucky, lucky man."

It took both women, one on each side, to get their patient safely in the patient chair. Too bad it didn't come equipped with seatbelts. Remmie raised her eyebrows at Carla. Noticing a gleam on her assistant's forehead beneath her blonde bangs, she had a pretty good idea the other woman was sweating as much as she was. Practically carrying a man through two rooms and lifting him into a chair was hard work. And that was even *before* the actual dental work began. Remmie took a deep breath as she slipped on her facemask, protective eyewear and disposable gloves. Here we go.

She held out her right hand. Carla handed her a cotton swab with numbing gel on the end.

"Okay, Mr. Ballentine. This gel will help ease any discomfort where I'll be numbing you. Open wide."

The man opened a half-inch. Hmmm. She'd need a whole lot more room to work with than that. She was restoring a molar for Pete's sake.

"Could I have you open a little wider, please?"

He closed his lips. Swallowed. And opened them again. The same half-inch as before.

Remmie eyed Carla, who picked up a small patient mouth mirror. The other woman slipped the mirror into Mr. Ballentine's mouth to help gently pry his jaws open. Even a little would help.

"Ack!" Their patient coughed and sputtered.

"Sorry," mumbled Carla.

They waited. He kept coughing.

"Do you need a drink of water?" asked Remmie.

"It wouldn't hurt." Cough. Cough. Hack.

Remmie sighed. She pressed the button on her side of the chair and watched as Mr. Ballentine's head rose higher and higher. As soon as he sat upright, she scooted her chair over to her sink and filled a blue plastic cup with water.

"Here ya go."

He took the cup and drained it.

Remmie held out her hand to take the empty cup. Time to get this show on the road.

He held on to it. "Did I ever tell you the story about my trip to the Grand Canyon?"

****

Mayor Bass was her first patient after lunch. That always made her nervous. She liked him, but there was always the chance that if she accidentally poked him in some way, he'd tell everyone in sight about it later on. You couldn't be too careful when dealing with a public official. They could be touchy.

She heard her front door open. She'd decided to wait in the back. The mayor would be here to monopolize her time soon enough.

"Hello, Carla!" he boomed.

Remmie winced. Why did the man have to talk so loud? It was amazing his wife had any eardrums left. Poor woman. Maybe that's why she took so many trips to see her grandchildren. Alone.

"Hi, Mayor," said Carla. "How are you?"

"Fine, fine. Is that cute little doctor ready for me yet?"

Remmie could picture Carla trying to hold back a laugh. For someone in the public eye, the man was more often than not unprofessional. But with no opponent in the last two elections, it didn't hurt his votes much. *Yes, the little doctor is ready, sir.*

Carla preceded the mayor to the back of the office where Remmie was waiting.

"Good afternoon, Mayor."

"Hello, Dr. Grin. Where should I park it?"

It? "Right here in this first chair will be fine." She pointed down.

He hoisted his hefty self down into the dental chair. Heaved a sigh. And looked at her expectantly.

She forced a smile. "Okay, then, let's get started."

"Yes, I have a meeting in forty-five minutes."

What? She cleared her throat. "Mayor, I'm sure Carla made it clear on the phone this procedure will take at least an hour and a half. We're doing a root canal after all."

The man frowned. "But this meeting is very important."

Remmie sighed. "Do you need to reschedule your dental appointment?" *We reserved an hour and a half of precious time for you, you dolt!*

"No, no. I want to get it over with, uh, no offense."

"None taken. We'll do the best we can, but it's not something we can rush."

He nodded. "Very well. Let me make a call."

"I'll get you numb first, and then you can call while you're waiting, okay?"

The man wasn't helping things. The more he talked to her, made calls on his phone, and insisted she should very well be able to do a ninety minute procedure in forty-five minutes, the more time they lost. She was good, but nobody could do it that fast.

Carla leaned back his chair, which creaked under his weight. She eyed Remmie over her mask.

Remmie, glad for her mask that hid her smile, raised her eyebrows back. She didn't dare look at Darcy. The younger woman was a giggle box at the worst possible moments.

"Okay, Mayor, first I'm going to place some topical gel on the spot where I'll be giving you the anesthetic. Open wide please."

Mayor Bass did indeed open wide. It was like a cavern. No wonder he talked so loud. His voice probably echoed on the way out. Helloooo down there....

"There. I'll leave the topical on for a minute, then we'll give you the rest."

After applying the gel, Remmie handed the soggy q-tip to Carla.

The mayor made a face. "That was awful. What flavor is that?"

Darcy glanced at the container on the counter. "Hmmm. That was coconut."

"Remind me not to have that kind again. What else is there?"

Remmie eyed the mayor. "We have gooey grape, but I didn't think you'd want that. That's what we normally use on the kids."

"Gooey Grape? Coconut? I think you need to have a better variety for your patients to choose from."

"I'll keep that in mind." Remmie kept herself from rolling her eyes. "All right, we'll get you numb, then I'll sit you up so you can make your phone call."

She held out her hand and Carla gave her a loaded syringe.

Mayor Bass looked at Remmie. "You won't hurt me, will you?"

"I'll do my very, very best not to. Remember, please don't move as I do this, that will give us a better chance of not causing you discomfort." *In other words, hold still or you might get poked.* Remmie calmed her nerves by taking a silent deep breath before inserting the needle. Pull out the cheek, Get finger situated on the handle of the syringe. Ease the needle in. *Easy. Easy.* Done. Whew!

"You okay Mayor?"

He squinted. "Well, I've had worse."

Remmie smirked under her mask. That was as close to a compliment as she would get from the man. She'd take it.

Remmie and Carla took of their masks, gloves and glasses. They left the operatory so their patient could make his phone call. He'd have several minutes to complete his business and also to get numb. Darcy stayed behind to clean up the other patient area. They returned to find the mayor asleep in the chair. Still sitting up. Remmie smiled at Carla.

Her assistant mouthed, "Afternoon siesta?"

Darcy whispered, "He snores."

After donning their masks and glasses again, they lowered his chair back down. The Mayor awoke with a snort. This was one of the many times in the life of a dental professional when wearing a mask came in handy. Honestly, how was she not supposed to grin at that? Wouldn't that make a great video for Youtube? He could use it for his campaign. Or…maybe not.

"Ready to get started, Mayor?"

"Yes, yes, let's get started. So I can get on with my meeting." He wiggled in the chair like a three-year-old.

"So you were able to get that taken care of?"

"Yes. All arranged."

"Good." She patted his shoulder. "I'm glad that worked out for you." Thank goodness. She didn't have all day to wait on him to conduct his business from her dental chair.

Since the man did possess the mouth-cavern, it was easier for Remmie to get in and do what she needed to. The tough ones were when a patient could only open the width of a thimble. Then Remmie had to practically stand on her head to see what she was doing. Especially if it was an upper molar. She really hated those. Too bad people weren't only equipped with lowers. Just her opinion. Probably wouldn't go over too well when people needed to chew.

Things progressed well. No surprises. No mishaps. Remmie heard the bell on the front door. She glanced at Carla. "We're not expecting anyone, are we?" This would not be a good time for an emergency patient with a toothache.

Carla shook her head. "Nope. Let me go see what's up."

Remmie used Carla's absence to take a break and stretch arms and shoulders. She rolled her head from side to side, loosening the knot that often formed in the back of her neck.

Carla returned. "Uh, Remmie?"

Remmie looked up. It wasn't often Carla called her by her first name in the office. Something must be up.

"Who was it?"

Victor appeared behind Carla. What was he doing here? In the patient area? Was he checking up on her technique or something? *Go away!*

The mayor turned his head. "Hello Victor. Glad you could make it."

Huh? Remmie lowered her eyebrows. What was going on?

Victor grinned. "Hi, Remmie. I have a meeting with the mayor. He suggested I meet him here since he's *stuck* in your dental chair."

Remmie fumed. It would have been nice if she were consulted about this beforehand. Of course, she would have said no. What could she do now? She couldn't stop the root canal midway through. And to yell at Victor in front of the mayor, or refuse in any way while in her official capacity in her office, would likely make the front page of tomorrow's Gazette. The Mayor was known for taking anything he viewed as a slight and blowing it to elephant proportions. She huffed out a frustrated breath.

Victor grabbed an operator chair from the next cubicle and made himself at home near the mayor's head. Which just happened to be right beside Remmie. What did he think he was doing? And she thought she was nervous working on the mayor before.

"Well, Mayor, I realize I'll have to do most of the talking since Remmie's hands are in your mouth."

Remmie glared at him. What a jerk.

"So hold up a thumb up or down for yes or no, all right?"

The mayor held up a pudgy thumb.

Remmie was seething beneath her mask. This could not be happening.

It took all of her concentration to do her job the best she could with Victor blabbing on and on about concerns he had about parking in front of his office. Even though it would affect Remmie too. Gee, it would have been nice to be included in the meeting. In an off sort of way, she was. But they hadn't originally included her. She happened to be doing *her* job during *their* meeting.

She wanted nothing more than to throttle Dr. Victor Barrett.

Chapter Five

Charles and Winston howled from the backseat. When Remmie glanced back at them, they both had their noses pressed against the cage door of their respective cat carrier. "It's okay, guys. Just a quick in and out of the office for your shots, okay? Then I have to get back to work." The howling increased. Deciding her voice wasn't keeping them calm, she kept quiet as she drove the rest of the way. She also should have known better than to use the word, 'shots.' Was she crazy? They knew what the s-word meant. The only time they went anywhere in the car was to go to the vet. She was sure that if they could have, they would have stolen her car keys so she couldn't take them anywhere. And locked her in a cat carrier.

Once in the parking lot, she juggled her keys, purse and the cats. Lugging both cat carriers at once was a chore. Especially since Winston weighed considerably more than Charles. She felt like a windmill with her blades stuck at uneven positions. By the time she got to the front door, she was breathing hard. "I have got to put you guys on a diet. Especially you." She looked down at Winston who gazed up at her with soulful green eyes. "Oh don't worry. I won't really put you on a diet. You'd eat my hand up to the wrist if I even tried." She took the purr from inside his carrier as an affirmation. Silly cat.

Right as she was ready to set down the carriers to open the door, a large hand reached in front of her toward the handle. She looked up to thank whoever it was for opening the door for her. She should have saved her breath.

Victor stood staring down at her. "Oh, it's you. I see you're an animal lover. I should have known."

"Yes, I am. Especially cats. Why? Aren't you?"

"You must be joking. They're noisy, messy and smelly. They're worse than kids. Well, no, probably equally as repugnant. I abhor all animals."

She glanced up at the sign above the door, which sported a giant cartoon dog and cat waving. "And I have no doubt they feel the same way about you. So then, why are you here? Did you get lost?"

"No. I didn't get lost. If you must know, I'm here to do some teeth whitening on a..." He turned his head away from her.

"What was that? Didn't catch that last part."

"A dog. A dog. I'm whitening a dog's teeth, okay? He's a show dog and the judges check that sort of thing." He shivered as if the whole idea gave him the willies.

"If you don't like animals, and don't want to whiten this dog's teeth, then why are you even here?" But before he could answer, she knew. "Ah, because the owner is paying you big bucks, am I right?" The man lived for money, and more money. How could she ever have been attracted to someone like him?

"Something like that. Plus, it will help me get the attention of all those new patients I'll take from under your nose."

"You're rude."

"No, what's rude is you making me stand here listening to the horrendous noise coming from those cages you're carrying."

"It's called purring. Haven't you ever heard it before? Never mind. That would be something pleasant, so of course you've never experienced it. Now, would you mind?" She tilted her head toward the door. Victor huffed out an irritated breath as he held the door for her.

Grin & Barrett

Remmie trudged in and set the carriers down on the marbled front counter. "Remmie Grin. I've got Charles and Winston for their check-ups." From behind her, she caught a snicker from Victor. She didn't bother to turn around. That would cause him to ridicule her further.

"It should just be a few minutes, Remmie."

"Thanks." She lugged the carriers toward the only available seat. Which, of course, was next to Victor. He sat there with his arms drawn to his sides and his hands inside his jacket pockets. He couldn't have made himself any smaller if he tried. The woman on his other side held the leash of her yorkie. The small dog yipped at him. He made a face. Was he afraid of the animals?

Just to vex him, she thrust one of the carriers toward him. "Hold this, will you? I need to get something out of my purse." She lowered her head so he wouldn't see her grin.

"B-but I-I," he sputtered as the carrier landed on his lap.

"Oh, don't be such a baby." She took Charles back from him and set him on the floor. Charles howled when he could see that Winston was sitting on Mommy's lap. Remmie put them both on the floor. They both howled.

"Can't you make them stop? It's awful. How do you stand that?" He covered his ears with his hands, like a little boy at a fireworks demonstration.

She raised her voice, making sure he heard her through his hands. "I can't hold both carriers on my lap, but if you'd hold one, they'd both be happy. Then they'd stop squalling." She smiled sweetly at him. That ought to do it.

"No, I couldn't," Right then, both cats screeched, increasing the volume. Victor's eyes grew large. "Okay, all right. Just give me one." He scrunched his face as if he stood in the middle of a sewage treatment plant. In the middle of summer.

"Victor, haven't you ever had a pet?"

"Never. My mom wouldn't let me. She said they were noisy and smelly."

"Well, I guess that explains why you don't like them. But honestly, you don't know what you're missing."

"I'll try to suffer through my disappointment."

"Remmie? We're ready for Charles and Winston." The assistant stood at the doorway to the examination rooms.

Remmie stood up with Winston. She eyed Victor. "Do you mind bringing Charles for me? It's hard for me to carry both. And I wouldn't want to make two trips, which I'm sure would irritate you even more." Although she'd love nothing better than that.

Victor grimaced. He stood with the carrier and held it out away from his person as far as possible. "If it will get rid of your furry rodents faster, by all means."

The dentists and the cats made their way to the room indicated by the assistant. Victor let out a sigh as he set his assigned carrier on the wide counter in the middle of the small room. Remmie set hers down next to it.

"Thanks Victor."

"Uh…sure." His face flushed. Hadn't anyone ever thanked him for anything before? No, probably not. It seemed he wouldn't normally do anything to be thanked for.

"See? You can be a reasonable facsimile of *nice* when you set your mind to it."

"How can you say that, Remmie? When I kiss you, you sure don't complain."

Oh great. He would bring that up *now*. Right when she'd decided to be immune to him. "Those kisses were a mistake. You caught me off-guard. At a weak moment. Very weak. Believe me, it won't happen again. I'm on to you now, Victor. I know what you're about." She crossed her arms, trying her best to look stern.

Victor leaned against the counter. "Remmie darling, you haven't a clue, have you? The chemistry between us cannot be denied." He smiled his big white-toothed grin and half-closed his eyes.

Remmie leaned away. He was coming in for another kiss! *Not on my watch, Mister.* Opening Winston's cage, she scooped the cat out and thrust him in front of her. Right as Victor's eyes were closing and he'd puckered his lips. .

"Aackkk! Ugh!" He blew cat hair out of his mouth.

Winston hissed.

Remmie giggled. "Don't feel too bad Victor. Winston didn't seem to like the kiss very much either."

Victor said something under his breath that she hoped he never voiced in mixed company. He stomped out of the room and slammed the door.

"Ah," she said to her cats, "that's the man we know and *don't* love."

****

Carla barreled in the office front entrance. "Rem, you will not believe this."

"What?" Remmie lowered the dental magazine she was reading.

"Read the advertisement section of today's paper."

Remmie smiled. "Does old man Hodges have another ad wanting someone to take his wife off his hands?"

"No. It's worse."

Remmie frowned as she took the paper Carla held out. On the back page, in large red letters was an ad. From Victor.

"Carla, he's advertising for new patients."

"I know."

She held the paper out towards Carla. "He's offering all initial services at half price."

"I know."

"What are we going to do?"

Carla shrugged. "I'm not sure. But I knew you needed to see that."

"Yep. You're right. I'm glad you showed me. I just don't know what to do about it, either."

The phone rang, startling them.

"Wow," said Remmie, "someone's calling early."

Carla took the call. When she was done, she didn't look happy.

"What?" Remmie was almost afraid to ask. This day wasn't starting out very well.

Carla replaced the receiver. "That was our first patient this morning."

"Uh-oh. Did Mrs. Liston's back go out on her again?"

"No. Mrs. Liston's back is fine. But she's switching dentists."

"Oh no. Don't tell me." *This can't be happening.*

"Yep, fraid so. She said she couldn't afford *not* to go to Dr. Barrett."

Remmie shook her head. "This is not good."

"Not even a little."

Four out of their ten patients for the day called with similar reasons for not coming in. Remmie knew she couldn't keep her business going if it continued for any length of time. Sure it was okay for now. For a few days, or even weeks. But she had a bad feeling about this. Victor was one determined, stubborn man. She couldn't see him stopping any time soon. He'd made it clear he'd do whatever it took to force her to sell to him. It seemed he had in mind to bankrupt her.

He had to be stopped. She needed a plan.

****

Remmie would love to avoid what she was getting ready to do. She hated speaking in front of people, even when she couldn't see them. Being interviewed by their local radio station now seemed necessary. Thanks so much, Victor Barrett. She'd written down some notes with answers to possible questions she anticipated the radio spokesman to ask. Taking a deep breath, she walked into the station.

The cute, twenty-something girl at the front counter smiled and pointed Remmie down to a door at the end of the hall. The sign on the door, "Quiet please, live recording in session" made Remmie's insides turn to mashed potatoes. She really didn't want to do this. She'd rather clean up fluoride vomit, as awful as that was. But she needed all the advertising she could get. And this was free. Free was good. When she'd learned the station was always looking for small businesses to interview, she decided she'd be an imbecile to refuse. Even though she was petrified.

She edged open the door, making sure to be quiet. A large bearded man in his fifties waved and pointed to a chair across from him. She eyed the microphone with distrust. Saying a quick prayer that she wouldn't yelp, sneeze, or burp on air, she took her seat.

The man smiled and introduced himself as Jim. Remmie was nervous about saying anything until she was sure it was safe from the sneaky microphone. She pointed to it and raised her eyebrows.

Jim laughed. "Don't worry, Dr. Grin. It's safe. Right now I've got a song playing. I'll let you know when it's time for your debate."

"My, uh, what?" Did he say debate? Oh no.

"Your debate. We decided since we had more than one request from a dentist, we'd combine them together for a debate. You know, to see who the better dentist is. Sounds like fun, huh?"

Remmie felt sick. No, this couldn't be happening. Why couldn't she come in, do her interview, answer a few questions and be on her way? Hopefully with lots and lots of free publicity that enhanced her tiny bank balance. Why did everything have to be so complicated?

The door opened. Victor came in. And stopped. "Hi, Remmie. Are you having an interview, too?"

Remmie scowled at him. "No, Victor, it seems they've decided we should have a debate. But I'm sure you already knew that." She'd like to pop him in his lying, scurvy mouth, but that wouldn't be smart in front of witnesses.

He shook his head. "No, I didn't. But, it's not such a bad idea, is it? It might be fun. You and I seem to do a lot of arguing anyway, right?" He grinned at her.

Jim said, "See? That's what we thought. It will be great."

Remmie wrapped her arms around her middle, as if that would keep her insides from exploding if her stomach kept revolting as it threatened to do right now. She pulled out her notes and put them on the counter in front of her. Skimming over them, she felt like she was cramming for an exam. She thought her dental school graduation had put an end to all that.

Victor leaned over to see what she was reading. "Cheat sheet, Remmie?"

Remmie snatched the paper off of the counter and stuffed it in her purse. "Just some notes that I thought might come in handy during my interview. Although now, it probably wouldn't help. Since it's a *debate*."

"Just be yourself, you two," said Jim "And you'll be great. The more natural you are on the air, the better the outcome."

Remmie smiled at Jim. But it took all she had not to upchuck instead. She just wanted this awful experience over and done. Now.

A production assistant came in to check the microphones. She adjusted both Remmie's and Victor's so they'd be more comfortable as they sat in front of them to talk. Remmie fidgeted in her chair.

Victor leaned over toward her. "Relax, Remmie. It will be fine. Be yourself."

"You don't know what you're saying, Victor. If I was completely myself at this moment, you'd be wearing a fat lip."

He wiggled he eyebrows. "You mean from all the kissing?"

"No. From me smacking you in your big mouth against your fake teeth."

"My teeth aren't fake, they—"

Jim whistled through his fingers. The noise was so loud Remmie jumped. "Doctors, save it for the debate, okay? We're almost ready."

Victor and Remmie glared at each other. Waiting. Because as soon as Jim gave the word, there would be no holding them back. The fur would fly. And Victor better look out, because as a cat person, Remmie was a fur expert.

"Okay, you two. It's time. I'll ask you some questions and you'll each get a chance to give your answers before we move on to the next one. Ready to go?"

Remmie nodded. Victor smiled at her. And not in a good way. Why was she thinking of a gargoyle? *Here we go.*

Jim turned up the volume on the latest song he'd played, fading it out when it was near the end.

"Okay, listeners, that was "Urgent" by Foreigner. Keep those song requests coming! But right now, we've got a special treat for you. During our series of interviews of small business owners, we've had people from retail, insurance, medical offices and locally owned banks. Today we have not one, but two local dentists. Who happen to have their offices right next door to each other. We decided to have them on at the same time, and to conduct an informal debate between them. Please welcome, Dr. Remmie Grin and Dr. Victor Barrett. Welcome Doctors."

Victor nodded toward Remmie, indicating she should go first.

Okay, Remmie, just don't throw up, faint, or explode. Putting a smile in her voice, she answered, "Thanks, Jim, for having me on your show."

"Yes, thank you Jim," said Victor. "Thanks for making time for small business owners like Dr. Grin and myself."

"You're both most welcome. Okay, before we get started, I'd like you each to tell us a little bit about how you got started in your chosen field."

Remmie decided she might as well go first. Victor was eyeing her, which probably meant that's what he wanted anyway. She nodded at him.

"Well, Jim, I've been a dentist here in town for seven years. It's a family practice, so I see adults and children both. I do pretty much any procedure anyone would need. Keeping within the confines of good health and what's best for the patient."

Jim smiled and nodded. He turned toward Victor. "And you, Dr Barrett?"

"Jim, I've been a dentist a while *longer* than Dr. Grin. I do all procedures, too, plus, Hollywood smiles. That's where I really shine."

Remmie rolled her eyes. For Pete's sake. What a spotlight hog.

Jim chuckled. "All righty then. Since we've set this up as a debate, I'll ask the questions and each of you will have a chance to answer. We always ask that our debate guests keep it clean. No profanity, please."

Remmie laughed. "I'm sure Dr. Barrett and I are more professional than that."

Victor nodded. "Absolutely."

"Okay," said Jim, "here's the first question. And I'll have Dr. Grin answer first."

Remmie smiled, still trying to talk her intestines from imploding or exploding.

"Dr. Grin, what would you do if a person came into your office in great pain, but had no money or insurance to pay you?"

"Hmmm. That's a tough one. Well, I'd at the very least take a look at them, snap an x-ray, and write them a prescription for antibiotics and pain meds until they could pay for an extraction. Otherwise, I'd send them to the emergency room. There they would get the care they needed even if they couldn't pay. I hate to say that, but if I did a free extraction for one patient, I'd have to be fair and do it for everyone. And unfortunately, that would put me completely out of business. Then I couldn't help anyone."

"All right, Dr. Barrett?"

Victor looked at Remmie and smirked. "I would handle it a bit differently than Dr. Grin. I'd most certainly see the patient, write them a prescription, and would also take out the painful tooth that's keeping them up at night."

Remmie scowled and shook her head.

"Got something so say, Dr. Grin?" asked Jim.

"No. It's just, no."

"We're here to debate. If you have an opinion about what Dr. Barrett said, this is the place to voice it."

"All right," she said, "since you put it that way. I don't believe Dr. Barrett is stating his intentions accurately."

"Are you saying he's lying?"

Remmie hesitated. "Well…"

Victor jumped in. "Now, wait a minute!"

"We're still on Dr. Grin, Dr. Barrett."

Victor sat back, crossed his arms, and fumed.

"Yes, if asked specifically, I'd have to say Dr. Barrett is misrepresenting himself."

"You mean he's—"

"Lying. Through his teeth." She folded her arms and gave a decisive nod of her head.

Victor was bouncing in his chair.

"Dr. Barrett, your turn for rebuttal."

"I cannot believe Dr. Grin would say such a thing. I'm a very good dentist."

"Yes, I'm sure you are, Victor," said Remmie. "No one is saying otherwise. That's not the question," said Remmie.

"And what makes you think, Remmie, that I wouldn't do exactly what I stated?"

"Money."

"Excuse me?" He stared at her.

"It wouldn't make you any money, so, no, I don't believe you would put that much time and effort into our fictitious patient."

"You're way off base, Remmie."

They glared at each other.

"Okay," said Jim. "Next question. And I'll start with Dr. Barrett."

Victor gave Remmie the evil eye and waited for his question.

"Dr. Barrett, what's the most important piece of advice you would give to a patient?"

Victor smiled as if the whole listening audience could see him. "Well, Jim, I'd have to say, only floss the teeth you want to keep."

Jim raised his eyebrows and laughed. "Well said."

Remmie's hand balled into a fist in her lap. What a bunch of doggy-doo.

"Dr. Grin, how about you?"

"I'd give pretty much the same advice, but in a more professional manner."

Victor narrowed his blue eyes at her.

Jim continued. "Dr. Grin, what do you do differently, patient-wise, when dealing with a child, as opposed to an adult?"

Remmie smiled. She found that the more they got into the debate, the less she worried about exploding intestines. "Kids are a whole different ball of floss, dentally speaking. When I talk to them, if it's their first appointment, or we're doing something different, or something that scares them, I kneel down on the floor next to their chair so we're at the same eye level."

Victor laughed. "You wouldn't have to kneel to do that."

"Dr. Barrett, it's not your turn yet."

Remmie glared at Victor, then smiled at Jim. "It's okay, I'm done with my answer."

"And you, Dr. Barrett? How do you handle dealing with a small child as opposed to an adult?"

"Well, Jim, I'd do everything Remmie suggested. But I'd also add that while I don't encourage parents back in the work area, I allow it just on the first visit with a small child. It helps them feel more secure."

He sat back and grinned. Remmie, remembering what he'd said about animals and children, knew he was probably making the whole thing up. Did he even see children as patients? She'd have to keep an eye out for that.

"Okay, Dr. Grin. Back to you. How do you feel about having another dentist move in right next door to your office? Does that upset you?"

Remmie's mouth fell open. That question didn't seem appropriate. She felt like she'd been set up. And that question wasn't like the others. How to answer? Be honest and say it sucked? Or go the nice route and fib. Nah. Honest was the way to go here.

"I'd have to say, Jim, that it came as quite a shock. I knew someone was moving in. And I knew it was a dentist. But I never dreamed it would be, uh..."

"Be what?" asked Victor.

This time Jim didn't interfere. Remmie glanced at him. He was smiling. He loved the friction between them. It was good for his ratings. She should have known this was too good to be true. *Free advertising my fat fanny.*

Remmie steeled her resolve. "I didn't know it would be someone who wanted to buy my practice."

Victor's mouth hung open. He seemed to regain control of himself and said, "Why Remmie, you know I only have the *best* intentions when it comes to your practice."

She rolled her eyes. "Give me a break. You've been after my practice from day one."

This time Jim interrupted. "From what I've heard, he's been after you for more than just your practice!"

"What?" asked Remmie and Victor in unison.

It became clear to Remmie that they had indeed been set up. What better way to get people to listen to your show, than to know they'd get a juicy earful when they tuned in? She crossed her arms, this time glaring at Jim. Victor did the same. Neither one spoke. *Let Jim stew in his own deceitful juices. The pig.*

Jim's face reddened. "Well, folks it seems our time is up for our debate. I'd like to thank Dr. Grin and Dr. Barrett for their time. Tune in tomorrow for our debate between two stay-at-home moms and their disagreement over what flavor of kool-aid they should serve their kids. Should be a real barn-burner."

The production assistant came in to help Remmie with her microphone. But Remmie had already unhooked the earpiece and was standing with her purse strap over her shoulder. Without a word, she turned on her heel and left the studio. She stormed out the front door, not even answering the receptionist when she said to have a nice day.

Outside, she fumbled in her purse for her keys. Why did they always disappear when she desperately needed to get in her car and drive away? *Now.*

Victor, who was parked beside her, walked up behind her.

"You okay, Remmie?"

She looked up and glared. Until she saw his face. He looked like he was concerned about her. But, that couldn't be right. Snakes didn't have feelings. Snakes only thought of themselves. And making money. Stupid, selfish reptiles.

"I'm fine. Guess that was a waste of time."

"Maybe. Maybe not. They say any publicity is good."

"Whoever *they* are, I'm not sure they meant something like this." She located her keys, got in her car, and backed out of the parking space. Out of the corner of her eye, she noticed Victor hopped away from the front tire of her car. That made her smile.

Chapter Six

Remmie knew Victor would be at the festival. There was no way she could ignore him. And as big a flirt as he was, he'd be surrounded by females old and young. She didn't get it. Okay, he was cute, in an evil, reptilian sort of way, but come on.... Was she the only one who could see through him? Beneath those perfect teeth was a competitive know-it-all. She'd seen it firsthand. How could anyone believe anything that came out of those lips? His luscious, kissable lips. *Stop it Remmie. What's wrong with you?* How could she think such traitorous thoughts?

As she strolled through the noisy, large crowd, she said hello to those she knew, and smiled at those she didn't. Although there weren't many of the latter. The town was small, and she'd lived there her whole life. Anyone who was a stranger didn't stay that way for long. Glancing around at some of the other women, she was relieved to see that her red v-neck t-shirt and white denim shorts fit right in with what they were wearing. She usually didn't worry too much about stuff like that, but for some reason, she was more aware of it since Victor came to town. But why should it matter? She didn't know why, it just did. Somehow his penetrating stare did something to her. Usually it made her mad, but…sometimes she felt something else. Attraction? No, that couldn't be it. How could she be attracted to the human version of a cottonmouth? Nevertheless, there was something. She just needed to figure out what that something was. And squash it. Till it was dead.

Mayor Bass caught her attention as he waved his pudgy arms and shouted to the crowd. "Okay, folks, let's have everyone line up for the watermelon eating contest. Right over here."

Remmie cringed as she headed that direction. Remembering Victor throwing that giant piece of fruit at her in the grocery store reminded her of what an idiot she'd been. Getting sticky with watermelon juice wasn't her first idea of something fun, but in this case, it was all for a good cause. All the money donated for activities went to the local library. Plus, she needed to keep in the public eye in a positive light as much as possible. With Victor trying to steal all of her patients, she had to stay vigilant. Her life was so much easier before he crawled into town.

She got in line to participate in the contest. They were having five people at a time sit at the red cloth-covered table. She wondered if the color choice was so the juice would blend in, in case the stains didn't wash out. Several groups of five had already finished, and the line was moving quickly. As Remmie watched the participants, she was amazed how fast some people could inhale a large piece of fruit. She wasn't kidding herself. There was no way she would win. It was a good show of community spirit for her to be involved. And of course, the whole Victor-stealing-patients thing. Couldn't hurt, right?

When she got up to the table, she took her seat at the far end. Where was everyone? She hadn't been paying attention to what was going on behind her. Too much daydreaming about Victor's kisses. Had she been the end of the line? Maybe she wouldn't have to go through with the sticky experience after all. Oh, well *darn*. She could at least say she tried.

Mayor Bass' loud voice boomed. "Well, folks, we're down to the last two people. Stay and root for your favorite dentist."

Oh no. As Remmie looked up, Victor walked up to the roped off area and sat down at the table. But not beside her. He made a point of sitting on the opposite end. He smirked at her. Why did he make her think of a cat with a mouse's tail sticking out of his mouth?

"Ready to lose, Dr. Grin?"

She shook her head. "Not on your life, Dr. Barrett. I'll be taking home the blue ribbon."

"Wanna bet?" asked Victor.

She thought they'd spoken low enough so no one else could hear, but several people from the front row of observers began to laugh. They must have passed on the fun, because soon the whole people-covered grassy knoll was cackling. Well isn't that just perfect?

One man in his fifties shouted out. "Who wants to bet Dr. Barrett will win?"

"Now, now," said the mayor, "you know we don't gamble in this town."

"Aw, just a quarter bet, Mayor. Just for fun."

The whole crowd, including Remmie and Victor, eyed the public official. "Well, since you put it that way...count me in for a dollar."

Remmie gasped. "Mayor Bass!"

Red-faced, the Mayor did an about face. "Uh...I meant, put me down for a dollar on Dr. Grin." He glanced hopefully in Remmie's direction.

Appeased, she nodded and smiled. Leaning over to Victor, she whispered, "That will show you not to go up against a hometown girl."

Victor waved her away with a flick of his long-fingered hand. "Please," he whispered back, "he's trying to appear kind to you. He has to. Isn't there a local election coming up this fall?"

Remmie eyed the enormous slice of pink watermelon on the plate in front of her. Wow. It was *huge*. And drippy. Glancing at her competitor, she noticed he had broken off a small piece. It was headed for his lips.

She pointed at him. "Hey. He's cheating!"

Victor lowered the piece of fruit. "Was not."

"Were too."

"Now, now," said the mayor, "we'll have none of that. Let's keep this a clean competition, Doctors." He looked at the timer set in the middle of the table. "Okay. Ready? Set? Go!"

Victor broke off a large chunk and chewed the end, holding a napkin under his chin to avoid a mess. Remmie shoved her entire face in hers. Even if she got fruit up her nose, there was no way she was letting him beat her. She inhaled piece after piece. Would all that watermelon hitting her stomach all at once cause an intestinal disaster later? No time to worry about it now.

Barely chewing, she was thankful watermelon was mostly, well, water. It slid down her throat without much effort. Until a large seed from the supposedly seedless watermelon stuck in her throat. Oh no. This is not good! She tried to swallow it, but it wouldn't budge. And the fruit in her mouth along with it now settled in her throat for a nice nap. An embarrassing rasp escaped her mouth.

Victor looked at her, as he broke off another piece. "Upchucking a furball, are we Dr. Grin?"

Oh no. The seed was not cooperating. She tried swallowing. Nothing. She attempted a cough, but couldn't even rummage one. Her eyes watered. She clutched her hands into fists, concentrating on getting the stupid thing dislodged before her head exploded.

"Look!" yelled a little boy in the front row. "Her face is all red."

A collective "Oh!" from the crowd forced all eyes on Remmie.

She heard an exaggerated sigh from her competitor. "Of all the ploys to get attention. Really, Remmie."

Still choking and panicking, Remmie caught movement from the corner of her bulging eye.

Victor now stood beside her, watermelon forgotten. "Remmie? Can you breathe?"

She shook her head. Victor's face swam in front of her. *Help, help, somebody! I don't want to die at the hands of a piece of pink fruit.*

Strong arms wrapped around her from behind. Large fists pushed in and up under her sternum.

"Ack! Accckkk!" The offending seed and a slimy mass of pink spewed out of her mouth, sailed over the table and splatted on old Mrs. Kerris' red and purple hat. The contrasting colors now residing on the hat were atrocious. Not to mention disgusting.

The little boy who'd originally pointed out Remmie's color to the crowd now pointed upward. "Eeewww! It's on her hat! On her hat!"

Remmie squawked a raspy cough. Oh no. How could this get any worse? Mrs. Kerris was one of her patients. Would the woman now defect to Victor's office after this incident? She looked up into the face of her rescuer. Victor's starched white teeth gleamed as he smiled.

"I'm so glad you're okay," he whispered. "You had me worried." Loud enough for the crowd, however, he said, "Everything *come out* okay, Remmie?"

The laughter swept through the crowd. Remmie narrowed her eyes at him as she wiped tears off of her cheeks. "Couldn't resist, could you? Had to make yourself look good."

"Frankly, Dr. Grin, you make that very easy for me." He leaned down to grasp her elbow.

"Just what do you think you're doing?"

"I thought you might need a little help getting up."

Grin & Barrett

She pulled her arm away. "I'm fine."

"Suit yourself. Since most of your watermelon is residing on that nice woman's hat, I guess that means I won the contest, though, huh?"

She pointed at him. "You're a rat."

"Hey, a step up from a snake."

"Oh! You...you."

"I told you not to call me a you-you." He put his hand on her shoulder. "Come on, Remmie, it looks like they're ready to clean up the mess here. Contest is over."

Remmie huffed out a breath and stood up. Without his help. There was no way, after the spectacle she'd provided, she would let Victor look like the hero again. She scooted up to Mrs. Kerris and apologized profusely. She headed toward the pasture where the three-legged race was starting. She was supposed to meet Carla there.

"Where are we going?" Victor shortened his long strides to match hers.

"What do you mean 'we'?"

"I thought since I saved your life and everything—"

Her head snapped up. She stared at him. "Saved my what?"

"You were choking. Don't you remember?"

She put her hands on her hips. "I suppose you'll be reminding me of that for the rest of my life."

"With any luck, yes."

He smiled at her. Why did that make her feel like a live chicken tied up over an alligator pen? Grrr.... she wanted to bite his nose off.

Oh, thank goodness. There's Carla. Her assistant waved both hands at her, trying to flag her down.

"Remmie. I just heard the weirdest thing, that you—"

"Choked on watermelon?"

Carla nodded. "Yes and that Dr. Barrett—"

"Saved my life?"

"Right. Are you okay?" Carla grabbed Remmie's hand.

Remmie nodded.

Victor sidled up beside Remmie. "Hello, Carla. How nice to see you again. Aren't you looking lovely?"

"Don't you try that crap on me, Dr. Barrett. Especially since you're the one trying to ruin Remmie's practice."

"Ruin is such a harsh word. I'd like to think I'm helping her out by offering her more money for her practice than it's worth."

Carla gasped.

Remmie held up a hand. "Carla, don't worry about it. He's full of beans."

"No," he said, "I'm full of watermelon. Speaking of which…"

"Oh no you don't, Victor. We're not turning this conversation around to make you look like the hero."

"But I am the—"

"Shut up, Victor." Remmie grabbed Carla's arm and propelled her toward the three-legged race.

The line for the race was long. Remmie was so glad to have found Carla. Now she wouldn't be subjected to being literally tied to Victor in another competition. Mrs. Bass, the mayor's wife, called the shots for the race. As a rather large woman, she had a voice like Minnie Mouse. The combination was disconcerting until people got used to it.

"All-righty people, let's keep this line in some kind of order. Line up single file, please, like little soldiers."

Mrs. Bass was also a kindergarten teacher.

Carla grabbed Remmie's arm as she slid behind her in line. "Rem, don't look now, but see that guy in the denim shorts and white t-shirt?"

Remmie turned her head towards the man.

"I said *don't* look now."

"How am I supposed to look if I can't look?"

Carla sighed. And blushed.

"Carla, you're as red as a beet. Who is he? What's going on?"

Carla stepped up beside Remmie and whispered, "That's Joe. He just moved back here and works for the new law office downtown."

Mrs. Bass' squeaky voice shrieked. "Ladies, please. How can we have order if you won't follow directions?"

Remmie's face grew hot. Hadn't she had enough embarrassment for one decade? Carla jumped behind her, but crouched down against her back, whispering again. "It's Joe. You know, Joe Hawkins?"

Remmie gasped. "No way. Creepy, skinny Joey Hawkins from the fourth grade?"

"He ain't creepy no more, sister," whispered Carla.

Remmie snuck another glance at the man ten people behind them in line. "Or skinny. Yikes. He's built."

"Oh, yeah," said Carla.

"You know, you two ladies don't have to whisper about me being built. I'm right here and I can hear you."

Remmie leaned back past Carla and glared at Victor.

"You again. What are you doing here?"

Victor sighed. "Must we go through this every time? I live here. I work next door to you. I saved your life. Ring any bells?"

Remmie turned her back to Victor and did her best to ignore him. He was like a stupid commercial jingle she couldn't get out of her head. Irritating. But at least she had Carla here to do the race with. Victor was on his own. *Ha-ha. Sorry about your luck.* Maybe Mrs. Kerris and her slimy hat would be his partner.

Carla poked Remmie's shoulder. "He's waving to me."

"Who?"

"Joe. Should I wave back?" Carla's eyes widened.

"Well, duh."

Carla stood there. Was she frozen in that position? Remmie grabbed Carla's other hand and raised it high, flopping it up and down. If Carla was too shy to wave, Remmie would help her along.

Carla snapped out of her stupor. "What are you doing?"

"Helping you meet Joe again."

"But I—" Carla pulled her hand away from Remmie.

"You don't want to meet him?"

"Well, yeah, but—"

"Carla, you're always teasing me about the dating pool. Isn't it time you took a dip?"

Carla blushed again. "Oh my gosh. Here he comes. He's walking this way."

Remmie looked toward the man striding toward them. Tall, blond, handsome. Although, not as handsome as Victor. *Ewwww. Where did that come from?* She really needed to get away from that man. For her own sanity. And the safety of her lips.

Joe reached them. "Hey, Carla, good to see you. And you're Remmie, right?"

"Right. Nice to see you Joe."

Joe focused again on Carla. "So, you gonna do this race?"

"Um, yeah."

He took a step closer. "Could I talk you into being my partner?"

Carla nodded.

Well isn't that peachy, thought Remmie, *now who will I—*

"So, Dr. Grin, it seems you need a partner for the race now."

Remmie glared at Victor. *Grrr.*

Grin & Barrett

The rope Mrs. Mayor Bass used to tie them together bit into Remmie's bare thigh. Most of the runners had the rope a little lower. Around their knees. But with Victor so much taller than Remmie, her section of the rope was just below her shorts. And inching upward.

Victor looked down at her. "Well, Shorty, ready for this?

She slugged him in the gut. "Don't call me Shorty."

His response was to hug her tight with his arm nearest to her.

She struggled against him. "Stop that. People are watching."

"So what? They've already witnessed how much you like me to kiss you."

Remmie balled up one first. "Oh, you insufferable—"

"Snake?"

"Yes. Snake."

He tilted his head towards hers. "You need some new nouns. That one's worn out."

"Okay. How about slime, cockroach, vermin?"

He shrugged. "Shows imagination. But keep working on it. I don't think you've captured the real me yet."

Oh, she'd like to *capture* him. Maybe in one of those big, painful bear traps.

When the starter gun fired, Remmie gasped and jumped straight up. Victor hauled her close to him, picking her up off of her feet with one arm, and took off running. Well, hobbling. Indignant, she scooted out of his grasp and attempted to keep pace with him. But how could a ladybug run with a granddaddy long-legs?

Her breath came in gasps. Her stride was half as big as Victor's. She glanced up at him. Why wasn't he gasping? He wasn't even sweating. And yet, her t-shirt was already sticking to her. Everywhere. Ick. Her left leg cramped where it was tied to Victor. Her thigh and his knee were almost even. But her thigh wouldn't bend like his knee could. How was that fair?

She looked at Victor again. Why was he grinning? He was looking at her shirt where it stuck to her chest. The cad.

"Eyes forward, *Vicky*."

"Did you just call me Vicky?"

"Did I stutter?"

Remmie felt nothing under her feet but air. Victor had once again lifted her and plastered her body against his.

"Hey." She squirmed against him. "Put me down."

"Nobody calls me Vicky."

He sailed past two sets of runners. Remmie had the fleeting thought that at least they might win the race. She clung to his arm with both hands. He was even speeding up. His long, muscular legs covered the distance quickly. Had he been a gazelle in a former life? He must have been a runner in high school or college. But, wait. Where was he going?

"Victor, the race is that way." She tugged on his shoulder, hoping to propel him in the right direction. He shrugged off her hand and kept going. Right towards a grove of pine trees.

"Victor? What are you doing?" Why was he going this way? The rest of the runners went that way. Uh-oh. He was out of his gourd. He'd finally snapped. Leaves snagged in Remmie's hair as Victor ran through the copse of trees. He didn't seem to notice that he had leaves in his perfect hair. He *had* lost it. Branches scratched the bare skin on her arms and legs. Ow!

"Victor. Stop! What are you doing?"

He slowed to a walk. "Nobody calls me Vicky." After another ten yards, he stopped walking. He lowered her to the ground.

Grin & Barrett

Remmie gulped in air as she tried to catch her breath. "Do we have an unpleasant memory of being called that, perhaps?"

Victor scowled. He was still looking down at her and not watching where he was going as he took a step. A very big step.

"Ahhhh!" Remmie was pulled off of her feet again. She felt wind whoosh against her face as they tumbled down the hill in one big tied-together lump. Arms and legs flailed and scraped against dirt and stone. She shut her eyes tight and clung to Victor, burying her face in his side until they stopped rolling. She was so dizzy. Ah. They'd finally slowed down and stopped. She smelled the grass as it tickled her nose and coughed out some dirt. And a little watermelon. She opened her eyes again. Why was it dark? *Oh no. Why couldn't she couldn't see?* Was she blind? Had she hit her head? No...wait. The large mass impeding her vision was breathing.

"Victor, you big oaf. Get off of me."

He rolled away. But took her with him because of the rope that connected them. Stupid, stupid rope. She was now lying on his chest.

His ice blue eyes stared up into hers. "What would you do if I kissed you right now?"

"I'd bite your nose. Now untie me."

He sighed and reached a long arm down to undo the knot. "There. You're free. Fly away."

Remmie scooted off of him and sat on the ground. Several feet away. "Why did you veer off the race path like that? Did the voices in your head tell you to?"

"I told you. No one calls me Vicky and gets away with it."

"That's it? That's the reason why? Gee if I'd known that, I would have called you Sally instead." She pulled a small twig from the left side of her hair.

"My Uncle Tobias used to think it was funny. He'd call me that if he thought I wasn't trying hard enough to win something or excel at whatever I was doing at the time. I guess he assumed he could goad me into trying harder. Doing better. Winning at all costs."

"Did it work?"

He sighed. "Yes. For a while. Until I grew up."

Remmie wrapped her arms around her knees and settled her chin on them. "Then what happened?"

"He came up with better incentives to entice me."

"Like…"

Victor frowned. "Do we really have to discuss this?"

"Not if you don't want to. But I figure you owe me since you tossed both of us down a hill. I'm going to have to invest in the band-aid market to cover all these scratches up. Do you happen to have a spare tourniquet in your pocket?"

"You could tell people you were attacked in your sleep by your cats."

"You're not answering the question, Victor."

He sat up and knelt on the grass. "I don't have a tourniquet."

"You know which question I meant."

He hesitated. Then shrugged. "Uncle Tobias is a dentist. A very successful one. He instilled in me a competitive spirit."

"Well, that explains a lot."

He glared at her. "And he's the one who footed my entire bill for dental school. I owe him."

"I see. So it's take no prisoners, win at all costs." Where did that leave her?

"Something like that."

She blew out a breath. "And stealing my patients falls into that category?"

"I wouldn't have to do that if you'd sell me your practice."

"Is he the reason you keep hounding me to sell?"

Victor sat back and crossed his arms over his knees. "I have no idea what you mean."

"He's got you over a barrel doesn't he?"

Victor looked away.

Remmie pointed at him. "That's it, isn't it? Because you owe him for school, he wants you to do this."

Silence.

"Victor, you don't have to do this, you know."

"He's not making me do anything. I...I want to do this."

She held out her hand. "But—"

"I owe him everything. If it weren't for him, I'd be…"

"You'd be what? A hippopotamus?"

He scowled. "No, I'd be nothing. A nobody. And most likely poor."

"There are worse things, you know."

"Not in my family."

"But—"

"Hey, they're down there!"

Remmie glanced up to the top of the hill. Half the town, it seemed, was staring down at them.

She winced. *This just keeps getting better and better.*

Chapter Seven

Victor folded his stack of just-dried underwear into neat, symmetrical squares. Wouldn't do to have wrinkly underwear. His uncle always told him he'd have a better day if his undies were unwrinkled. Victor didn't know if he'd have the same kind of day if they looked liked he'd run over them with his car. He'd never put it to the test. But since his uncle was so successful, there must be something to his advice.

He placed the pile in his shiny, white plastic laundry basket and headed for one of the dryers he'd set on low, to retrieve his dark shirts and jeans. If they had a few wrinkles, he could always iron them at home. He'd be glad when his new deluxe washer and dryer set was delivered. The Laundromat seemed to attract some people who seemed a bit crass. Didn't they understand laundry etiquette? He still couldn't believe the one woman who shrieked at him when she thought he'd stolen the dryer she'd been using. As if he would ever do something like that. The hillbilly.

A tiny bell sounded when someone else came in the door. He didn't bother looking up. He might get shrieked at again. No thanks. He still had goose bumps from the first time. That was one large, scary woman. Better to stand quietly and fold his jeans. He only half-listened to the conversation between the newcomer and someone across the room.

"Hey, Doc."

"Hi Ann. Feelin' okay?"

"I'm still kind of sore where you took the tooth out. But thanks again for getting me in your office today."

Grin & Barrett

"No problem. Glad to help."

Victor whipped his head around. Ah. So Dr. Grin was a Laundromat girl. Good to know. Maybe it wasn't so bad he had to use the facilities for a while. Abandoning his pile of jeans, he leaned against a dryer and watched her lug her giant orange duffel bag to the nearest washer. He was sure she hadn't noticed him yet. If she had, she wouldn't be this calm. She'd be calling him a snake or a you-you. He chuckled. She was so darn cute. He'd much rather date her than do business with her. Too bad he had to bug her until she sold him her practice. Victor sighed. Uncle Tobias would have his head if he didn't come through.

Remmie reached her short arm into the giant bag. She was up to her armpit. She must still not be able to touch stuff at the bottom, because as Victor watched, her head and shoulders disappeared into the bag, as well. Might as well make himself useful.

"Need some help?"

"No I—" came from inside the bag. "Wait... Victor is that you?"

"Would you prefer someone else?"

"If you could arrange it, yes." Her head popped out of the bag.

Victor bit his lip trying not to laugh.

"What? Is my hair messed up?"

Her hair, having rubbed the inside of the slick vinyl bag, had enough static electricity to power a large generator.

"You could say that."

"Oh. You're saying that so I'll check it out. Then you can say 'made you look'."

"Yes, because every man over the age of eleven does that on a daily basis."

She snatched her purse and dug out a compact mirror. "Oh, for Pete's sake. Would you look at that mop?"

"You look like a character from Sesame Street. Do you remember Snuffalupagus?"

"You're a—"

"Remember, you need some new nouns."

"Weasel," she said between gritted teeth.

"Better. At least we're getting to some creatures with fur instead of scales. You've made my day, Dr. Grin."

"Why are you here?" She found a comb in her purse and performed damage control.

"Do we have to start every conversation with a question like that?"

"I mean, why are you at a Laundromat? I'd think with all of your riches from stealing other dentist's patients, you could afford your own appliances."

"Of course I can afford them. They just haven't arrived yet. Well, why are *you* here?"

"My washer is being repaired." She put her hands on her hips. "You know, Victor, I'm still floored that you're taking my loyal patients away from me. Who does something like that?"

"For starters, how loyal can they be if they jump ship? And you know good and well why I'm doing it. You need to sell me your practice. If you wouldn't fight it so hard, you'd see I can offer you a very nice deal."

"I don't want your nice deal, Victor. I want my own practice. The one I've built from nothing. The one I haven't had any help from anyone with. Even though my dad and brothers said I could never do it. I'm proud of what I've accomplished. Why can't you respect that?"

"Oh, I respect it. But I still need to buy your practice."

"You're impossible."

He grinned at her with his snow-white crowns.

"So who glued on those fake white teeth for ya? Your barber?"

"Remmie, what a terrible thing to say. My Uncle Tobias created my Hollywood smile if you must know. And for the record, my barber is extremely gifted. But just with hair." He reached up and touched his hair, as if paying it homage.

Remmie rolled her eyes. "Oh good grief. You're such a girl."

"Excuse me?"

"You care more about your appearance than any woman I know."

"That's not true." He placed his hands on his hips, impatiently tapping one foot.

"And I don't know of any other man around here who gives that much thought to how he looks."

"Well maybe they should. It's uncivilized to be otherwise."

Remmie laughed. Which turned into an unladylike snort. "Oh Victor, if nothing else, you're entertaining."

Victor enjoyed hearing Remmie laugh. Even though it was at his expense. He'd love to kiss her right now. But he'd get a black eye if he tried. Was she serious about her father and brothers not believing in her? He guessed he could identify. Uncle Tobias sure made him fight for every scrap he got.

Still, his uncle had given him so much. He never would have been able to attend dental school on his on steam. Financially or academically. A few well-placed calls from Tobias to his golf buddies, who also happened to run the school, sure didn't hurt any.

He watched Remmie as she upended her huge duffel bag and a clump of wadded clothes tumbled out. Opening the nearest washer, she grabbed a handful of clothes and dumped them in, followed by a half-cap or so of detergent. Slamming the lid, she stepped to the next washer. Repeating the cycle, she loaded four washers before she ran out of clothes.

Remmie looked up at Victor. "What?"

"Do you always do that to your clothes?"

"Do what? Wash them? Well, yeah. Otherwise they get moldy."

He shook his head before she'd even finished talking. "No, Remmie. You're ruining your clothes."

"No, I'm not." She pulled the knobs on each of the washers to start the cycle.

"You treat them like garbage. Grabbing a wad of them, stuffing them in the machine. Dumping an unmeasured amount of detergent in on top. You're not even separating your lights and darks. You need help. Serious help. Lucky for you, I can give it."

Remmie rolled her eyes. "I do not believe this. I'm getting a lesson in laundry from a man who has his hair done by a nibbling rat."

"I'm choosing to ignore that last comment in the interest of helping you out."

"How magnanimous."

Victor smiled. "Why thank you. Now, the first thing you need to do is—"

She held up her hand in front of him, nearly touching his nose. "Stop. I am not going to stand here and listen to you lecture me on how to wash my clothes. I've been doing it myself for a very long time, and they haven't fallen apart, evaporated, or exploded. So, take your lecture and stuff it up your—"

"Dr. Grin, Dr. Barrett. How nice to see you."

Remmie turned her head toward the man waddling toward her. "Hello, Mayor."

"Nice to see you, Mayor," said Victor.

"Now why is it every time I see you two you're always together? Something the rest of the town should know? Hmmm?" He rubbed his chubby hands together.

"No!" Remmie shouted. "I mean, uh, no, there isn't."

Grin & Barrett

Victor stared down at Remmie. "Oh come on, *honey*, don't be shy. Go ahead and tell him." He slipped his arm around her shoulders. That should get her going.

Remmie's face turned red. "Tell him what?"

"Well now," said the mayor, "I had a feeling about you two."

Remmie gritted her teeth until the public official had wandered off to yap at someone else. She whipped around to glare at Victor, throwing off his arm. "What have you done?"

Victor smiled and shrugged.

"Now the whole town will think we're…"

Victor placed his hands on Remmie's shoulders again. "Think we're what? Involved? Engaged? Married?"

Remmie's eyes opened wide. "Ahhhh!" She stormed off to check on her laundry.

Victor grinned. Maybe this was a good thing. If everyone assumed he and Remmie were involved, it would make it that much easier for Victor to kiss her in public. Yes, a very good thing indeed.

But he was still determined to teach the woman Laundry 101.

****

Remmie stood guard outside her office door. If she lost one more patient to Victor…grrr. She'd like to poke him in the eye. Maybe if she could waylay some of her patients who had defected to the dark side, she could convince them to come back. Couldn't they see that she was the better dentist? And for that matter, the better human being? Why couldn't they see past his fake white teeth to the real Victor Barrett?

"Hello. Dr. Grin."

Remmie looked up to see a deliveryman holding a large box. "Hi. For me?"

"Yep. Want me to take it in for you?"

"Thanks, that would be great."

She escorted him back to the door, had him set the box down in the foyer, and then scooted the box behind the front counter after he left. Didn't need someone tripping over it and suing her. It was a huge box. She couldn't imagine what Carla ordered. Because Remmie hadn't ordered anything in that large of a quantity for quite some time. And it wasn't in Darcy's job description.

When she went back outside to her post, Victor was there. Smiling. At Remmie's first patient of the day. Her eyes widened. *Oh!* She'd only been gone for three minutes. The man didn't waste any time.

"Dr. Barrett, it seems you've met *my* patient, Mrs. Tolliver."

"Why yes, we were just getting acquainted. I was telling her how much I liked the fragrance she was wearing. But then she told me what wasn't wearing any perfume. Can you imagine my surprise?"

Remmie crossed her arms. "Oh yeah. I can imagine all sorts of things." She turned to her patient and smiled. "Ready for your appointment?"

"Well I—" Mrs. Tolliver turned toward Victor who was holding her hand in both of his.

Victor winked at Remmie and turned toward the older woman. "It was so nice to meet you Mrs. Tolliver. Have a lovely day."

Remmie smirked at Victor as she opened the door for her patient.

Victor moved up behind her and whispered, "Well played, Dr. Grin. Until next time." He bent over in a low mock bow.

Remmie scurried into her office. Time to remind her patient why *she* was the better choice of dentist.

Her morning progressed nicely. All of her patients showed up. No thanks to Victor. She had a few minutes before she headed out for lunch. Maybe she could unload the box that was delivered. Although she still didn't remember ordering anything recently. She grunted and pulled, tugged and sweated, situating the box so she could kneel in front of it on the floor.

She leaned down to read the logo. Homefront Spectacular Gifts. Hmmm. She was *sure* she'd remember if she'd placed an order with them. Their stuff was pretty pricey. She didn't usually order much from them.

"What'cha got there, Rem?" Carla bent down to peer at the box.

"I was hoping you could tell me."

"Nope. I didn't order from them." She placed her hand on her boss's shoulder. "Wait a minute. Look at the address label. It just says 'Dental Office', but the address is one number off."

"You're right. This is for…Victor. Do we dare?" She placed her hand on one of the flaps, ready to open the box.

"Oh, we dare, all right."

Remmie used a box cutter to tear away the tape that held the flaps in place. "Carla, look at this."

Inside were stacks and stacks of sterling silver picture frames, jewelry, wristwatches and video games. Remmie looked at Carla. "What in the world?"

"Isn't it a little early for buying Christmas gifts?"

Remmie frowned. "Yes, but not for buying bribery gifts."

"You really think…?" Carla's mouth dropped open.

"Yeah. I really do. The jerk is *buying* patients. Even for kids. Look at all those video games."

Carla's eyes widened. "Remmie, that man is a snake."

"You're preaching to the choir, Carla."

****

It was dental awareness week at the local elementary school. Remmie was asked to participate. And she assumed they'd asked Victor, too, of course. She sighed. He seemed to be everywhere she was these days. She felt like a character in Mary Had a Little Lamb. *And everywhere that Remmie went, the dentist was sure to follow.*

With Carla's help, Remmie loaded up her trunk. Carla was staying at the office to cover the phones, even though they hadn't scheduled any patients that morning. They had tiny toothbrushes, small floss picks, bubblegum flavored tubes of toothpaste, and Remmie's lion hand puppet, Renaldo. Kids seemed to pay more attention when Renaldo did some of the talking.

On the short drive to the school, she admired the pink and purple petunias in hanging baskets on front porches of older homes. Yellow daffodils graced many yards. And several people were out mowing thick green grass in their front yards. She'd always put off a garden, but maybe it was time to plant some flowers in wooden barrels in front of her office. Couldn't hurt. As long as Victor didn't drag the barrels over in front of his office and take credit. She could see him doing something like that.

Victor was getting out of his sports car when Remmie drove into the visitors' parking lot.

"Hi Remmie. Thought I'd see you here. It must be your lucky day, huh?"

Remmie rolled her eyes. "Oh, sure."

He had one box under his arm and held out the other one. "Want me to carry that for you?"

"No. I have it. Thank you." Why couldn't he just go on in? Did he have to walk in with her?

He shrugged. "Suit yourself."

"I always do."

"That's for sure."

She frowned. "What's that supposed to mean?"

Victor opened the door to the school. "Shh. Someone might hear us in here."

"Did you shush me?"

"You mean you're not sure? Here let me do it again." He pursed his lips.

She held out one of her hands to stop him. She dropped the box. "Rats."

"Shh."

"Stop shushing me, Victor."

Remmie bent down to grab the box. It slipped out of her hands and fell upside down.

Victor raised his eyebrows. "You might want to be careful. Did you have the lid shut tight?"

Remmie glared at him. "Do I look like an idiot?"

He grinned.

"Shut up, Victor."

"I didn't say anything."

She pointed at him. "Your expression said it for you."

He smiled at her and closed his eyes halfway. "What does my expression say now?"

He wanted to kiss her. "Back off, Mister."

"Very good. That's exactly what I was thinking."

Remmie grabbed the box and tried to stand up. The lid popped off. All the little toothbrushes, floss and paste fell on the floor. Thankfully, they were all individually wrapped. She scooped up handfuls at a time and tossed them in the box.

She looked up at Victor. "Well are you going to help me or not?"

"I thought you didn't want my help."

She frowned.

He held up a hand. "Okay." He crouched down and scooped items off of the floor.

Once everything was back in the box, Victor began to rearrange the items.

"What on earth are you doing?"

"Everything is jumbled. You'll feel much better after all similar items are together."

"I don't give a rat's patoot about that."

He clicked his tongue. "Such language."

"We're going in the rooms and handing these out to the kids. The box will be empty. So what does it matter?"

He shrugged. "Just trying to help." Once she stood up and had a firm grip on the box, Victor put his arm around her shoulders.

"Stop that."

"I thought since you wanted my help—"

She squirmed until he moved his arm away from her. "Not that kind of help."

He grinned at her and opened the first classroom door they came to. Mrs. Jenkins' first grade class.

The teacher waved them in and smiled. "Okay class, it's time for our lesson on dental health. Two of our dentist friends are here to help us today." She held out her hand and shook Remmie's. "So nice to see you again, Dr. Grin."

"Thank you, Mrs. Jenkins."

The teacher reached her hand out to Victor. "And I don't think we've met before."

He took her hand and gave his flirty grin. "No we haven't. I'm Dr. Barrett. Very nice to meet you." Remmie rolled her eyes. Was the teacher actually blushing? Good grief.

A little red-haired boy in the front row raised his hand.

Mrs. Jenkins turned to him. "Yes, Donny?"

"You've never met that man before, but you said he was our friend."

She smiled. "They're our friends because they are dentists."

He raised his hand again. "But my mom and dad said dentists are mean. And that they always hurt you."

Remmie inwardly groaned. *Oh perfect. So this was how it was going to be. Better get out the puppet.* She reached into the box and drew out Renaldo. Twenty-three pairs of eyes were immediately focused on the lion. She reached back into the box and grabbed a giant pink plastic toothbrush.

Eleven little hands shot in the air.

"What's his name?"

"Is he soft?"

"Does he bite?"

Remmie laughed. "His name is Renaldo. His fur is very soft. And he does not bite."

A little girl with blonde curls and large green eyes raised her hand. "Can we pet him?"

Remmie looked at Mrs. Jenkins.

The teacher answered. "After we learn all about how to take care of our teeth, I think we could form a quiet, straight line and all get to pet him."

Remmie demonstrated how to hold the toothbrush and instructed them to brush in circles at the gums. Renaldo didn't possess teeth, but Remmie had discovered that didn't matter to the kids. Their attention was on Renaldo and the fact that he had a toothbrush in his mouth. That was the main idea. If they grasped any further concepts at this age, it was all gravy.

After Remmie went over brushing and flossing, she looked at Victor. Was he going to say anything? Or was he leaving this all up to her? He was just going to stand there like a giant piece of eye-candy. Which, he did very well. But still….

Mrs. Jenkins clapped for Remmie, indicating the class should do that same. Tiny hands beat together in exaggerated clapping. Remmie placed Renaldo back in the box and stepped off to the side. She smirked at

Victor. Did he even have anything to say? It wasn't like he could go over brushing and flossing again. And there was no way she was letting him borrow Renaldo. She watched in amusement as he bent down and opened his box. He'd also brought toothbrushes, floss and toothpaste. But what more could he have in there? He'd already told her he didn't like little kids. He wouldn't have his own puppet, she was sure.

From inside the box, Victor produced a green cloth bag. Untying the drawstrings, he pulled out five rubber balls the size of baseballs. Red, blue, yellow, orange, and green. He turned toward the kids and grinned.

"Okay, cats and kittens, I need your help for the next part."

Cats and kittens? What was this, 1962?

"Every color is a word. First I'll tell you what each one means, and then you can help me by calling out the words."

Remmie's eyes widened. What in the world was he doing? Was this Victor? The sarcastic, doesn't-like-kids-or-animals, Victor? She watched the kids. Their eyes were glued to Victor. Especially when he started juggling the balls. Juggling?

"All right." He stopped juggling and put all the balls on Mrs. Jenkins's desk. "We'll start one by one. Dr. Grin will help me."

Remmie stared at him. *I will? Since when?*

He smiled at her with perfectly white teeth. "Okay, Dr. Grin, I'm going to call out a color and you're going to throw it at me."

"*At* you?"

"Well, *to* me."

She smirked and nodded. He knew as well as she did she'd prefer to pitch a hard ball upside his head.

"Get ready Dr. Grin. Okay. Throw me the…red one."

Remmie glanced down, fumbled for the correct one, and then picked it up. She lobbed it to Victor, and he tossed it up and down in the air.

"Okay kids, red is for brushing. Can you say it with me? What's red for?"

"Brushing!" the kids yelled.

"Excellent. Dr. Grin, throw me the…blue one."

Remmie tossed it, but not very well. Victor caught it though, and started to juggle the two rubber balls."

"All right," he said to the class. "Blue is for flossing. What's blue for?"

"Flossing!"

"Next one Dr. Grin. Throw me the….let's see, the yellow one."

Remmie tossed it. Much better that time. At least she was keeping it in the room.

"Kids, yellow is for toothpaste. What's yellow for?"

"Toothpaste!"

"Next, Dr. Grin, I want the…green one."

Remmie lobbed it. Victor kept juggling. Remmie still couldn't believe it. Victor. *Juggling.* She would have been less surprised if he'd thrown the ball *at* the kids.

"Kids, green is for eating fruits and vegetables. What's green for?"

"Eating fruits and vegetables!"

"And the last one, Dr. Grin."

Remmie tossed it underhand, but not very well. It missed Victor and bounced on the floor. The kids giggled.

Victor grinned at her. "Let's try that again."

Remmie, embarrassed, retrieved the ball and tossed it, gently, to Victor. Without effort, he caught it and incorporated it into his juggling. Remmie was impressed. Although, she'd never tell him that.

"And the last one. Orange is for…visiting your dentist. What's orange for?"

"Visiting your dentist!"

"You guys did great," said Victor. "Now Dr. Grin will help me one last time."

Remmie looked at him. There was more? Hadn't she helped him enough?

"Okay, Dr. Grin, if you would, please grab that green bag and hold it open."

Remmie did as instructed, although it galled her to have to follow his orders just because they were in front of a bunch of little kids with big ears. She felt like his minion. It would have been nice to have been forewarned about this. She opened the bag.

"Okay," said Victor. "Now hold it out toward me."

Remmie held it out. Victor, while still juggling, tossed the balls one by one, until they were all in the bag. Victor grabbed Remmie's hand and pulled her down in a bow in front of their audience. The kids clapped and laughed.

Victor leaned toward Remmie. "Guess we were a hit."

Remmie was still in shock.

On their way out of the school, Remmie was shaking her head.

"What?" asked Victor.

"Juggling?"

He shrugged. "I learned how to do that in high school."

"You had a class in juggling? What school did you go to? Clowns-R-Us?"

"It just so happens I learned that in Drama Club."

"Ah, now it makes sense."

"What makes sense?"

"You do seem to like all the attention. I guess that goes with being a drama queen."

"King." He glared. "And by the way, Remmie, you made a very astute assistant."

"I am not an assistant. I am a dentist. There is a difference."

"I only meant—"

"I know what you meant. And don't ever pull anything like that on me again without warning. Got it?"

Victor nodded. "I don't think I'm the only one with a gift for the dramatic."

"You are a—"

He held up a hand. "Remember, need some new nouns."

"Virus."

"Not what I expected. But interesting none the less. Remmie, I think you're starting to like me."

Remmie threw her empty box in her trunk, wrenched open her door and climbed in then squealed her tires on the way out of the parking lot. The nerve of that man!

Chapter Eight

Remmie could not have heard her assistant correctly. "But Carla, you don't want me with you on your date with Joe."

"I'm so nervous, Rem. I haven't been on a real date in so long. What will we talk about?"

Remmie leaned back against the front counter. "You're going to a movie. You won't have to talk much. For at least two hours, you can just sit and watch the screen."

Darcy frowned. "How long has it been Carla? Geesh, I go out almost every weekend."

Carla scowled at the younger woman. "That's because I'm no longer twenty, Darce." She turned back to Remmie. "Please say you'll go."

Remmie shook her head and sighed. "I'll go, but I don't think it's a good idea. What will Joe think when you bring me along?"

Carla frowned. "Well, why don't you just *happen* to show up? I'll make sure the seat next to mine is empty. Then you can come in and—"

"Act like I just happened to be at the movies? Alone? That's going to help my self-esteem."

Darcy shook her head, her long red ponytail bouncing. "That's lame."

Remmie crossed her arms and raised her eyebrows at Darcy.

Carla touched Remmie's shoulder. "Oh, Rem, I know it's a lot to ask."

"No, Carla, It's not. You're my best friend. Of course I'll help you."

Carla bent down to hug her. "Thank you so much. You won't regret this."

Remmie walked back toward the patient area. *Oh, I don't know about that. I have a very bad feeling about this.*

****

The line for the movie was long. Remmie stepped up onto the sidewalk from where she'd had to park on the street. The lot had been full. This was not good. How would Carla be able to hold a seat for her? It wouldn't do much good if they sat ten rows apart. Kind of defeated the whole purpose.

By the time Remmie got her ticket and made her way past the throng at the concession counter, she rushed down the hall where the theaters were located. She felt as if she'd walked a quarter mile by the time she found it. She stared at the movie poster outside the door. Oh no! She couldn't do this. The picture showed a man wearing a ghoulish mask holding a knife to the throat of a beautiful blonde. It was a slasher move. Remmie didn't do slasher movies. Carla *knew* that. Remmie sighed. She'd promised Carla she'd be there, and she would go, but boy oh boy was her friend going to owe her. Big time. If she ended up with nightmares, Carla would be getting calls in the middle of the night.

The lights were going down when she got up enough courage to enter the theater. Even the music for the beginning credits was frightening. Her skin crawled. The hair on her arms stood on end. *Oh Carla how could you?*

She tried to locate Carla and Joe by standing in the back and scanning the packed house. No luck. She held her purse close to her body, still shivering from the creepy music, and started down the left aisle. She was halfway down when she heard Carla's high-pitched giggle. There. She'd finally located her. Oh come on. The first row? At a horror flick? Carla was going to owe her a month's worth of her favorite chocolate bars, her favorite frozen ice cream concoction at the Dairy Barn, and twenty of her famous shoulder rubs after a hard day of bending over patients. At least. And this guy better be worth it.

When she reached the row, the seat next to Carla was taken. Of course. There were three seats near the end, but she knew Carla wanted her closer than that for moral support. If someone sat between them, they might not appreciate the two leaning in front of them so they could have a conversation.

Her friend was engrossed in what her date was saying. Remmie couldn't seem to get her attention by waving her hand. Or clearing her throat. Or calling her name. Repeatedly. So much for moral support. At this point, Remmie might need some. Joe spotted Remmie. He nudged Carla. She turned her head.

"Oh, Remmie, what a surprise."

Remmie clenched her teeth. Her friend was an even worse actress than she was. "Hi guys. How are you?"

Carla looked at the seat next to her. Her face fell. Obviously she hadn't been paying attention when someone else tried to sit there. Remmie raised her eyebrows at Carla.

"Excuse me," Carla said sweetly to the woman to her left. "My friend just showed up unexpectedly. Would it be too much to ask for you to move over one so she could sit by me?"

The woman, a good sport, smiled and stood. "Not at all." She moved over two spaces. Did she think Remmie was too chubby that she might need more than one seat? Remmie thanked her and scooted past her. She sat down hard with a harrumph and stared at Carla.

"What?"

"A horror flick, Carla?"

Carla lowered her eyebrows. "Huh?"

"Carla, it's a slasher movie."

"It is?"

Remmie's eyes widened. "You didn't even notice?"

"I, uh, well no." She turned red. "I guess I was, um…"

Remmie sighed. "Never mind. I know you didn't do it on purpose."

Carla grabbed her hand. "No, of course not. And," she whispered, "thank you."

"You owe me, girlfriend."

"Oh trust me. I know."

Remmie put her purse on her lap, but didn't let go of it. Her fingernails dug into the brown leather of the strap. Her heart pounded. Her mouth went dry. And the movie hadn't even officially started yet. She heard conversation to her left. The Good Samaritan woman had a date who'd finally shown up. Well good for her. She had a date. Carla had a date. Remmie had her purse. What was wrong with this picture?

As the first scene opened with a large man skulking around a woman's bedroom window, Remmie felt something touch her arm. She jumped. Her head whipped around. Light from the screen illuminated the side of a man's face as he sat down next to her. Not just any man. Victor. Of course.

"What are you doing here?" she asked.

"Watching a movie. Isn't that why we're all here?" He positioned a small, red and white striped box on one knee and placed a large white cup in the holder between their seats.

Remmie sighed. "But why do you have to sit *here*?" *Right here.*

"Well, that's easy. When I got here there was only one ticket left for this movie. The usher showed me to the last seat left in the theatre. Imagine my surprise when it's this one. Right here. Next to you."

Remmie groaned. "What have I done to deserve this?"

The Good Samaritan woman shushed her.

"Popcorn?" Victor held out his box.

"No. Thank you."

"Soda?" He picked up his cup and angled the straw toward her lips.

"Thank you, no. You might have some disease I'd rather not contract."

"But you've already kissed me. More than once. Don't you think—"

They got shushed again.

Victor leaned over and whispered in her ear. "Isn't this cozy?"

She whispered back. "Go away."

"Sorry Darling, this is literally the only seat left."

"I'm a lucky, lucky girl."

"Why, thank you." He scooted over and put his head on her shoulder.

She shoved him away.

He put his arm around her.

She pinched his hand.

He tried to kiss her cheek.

She bopped him in the ear.

The scary music intensified. As much as Remmie did not want to watch the screen, her eyes were drawn there. From the front row, they were sitting so close she had to crane her neck to look up. The villain was sneaking up behind the heroine. Closer. Closer. Light reflected off of the blade of the huge, serrated knife. The scary man sneered. He raised the knife high in the air above the woman's head. He was going to decapitate her! Remmie's hands twisted her purse straps into a knot. *Turn around, lady. He's got a knife. Run. Run!*

Victor blew in her ear.

Grin & Barrett

"Eeeeekkk!" Remmie jumped straight up in the air and landed somewhere to the left of her seat.

Twenty-nine people yelped and shushed them. Victor's drink flew in the air and landed on the lap of the man directly behind them. The guy cursed. Loudly.

Remmie glanced at the man. "Sorry," she muttered. She looked down at her lap. It was covered in popcorn kernels. She sighed. Now she'd have greasy stains on her favorite jeans to try to remove. Maybe she'd have Victor do it. He seemed to think a lot of his laundry skills.

Victor pulled her close. "Remmie, I know you like me to kiss you, but you must really have the hots for me. I mean, we are in a public theatre, you know."

Remmie glanced down again. She was on his lap! How did that happen? "Ahh." She popped back into her own seat.

Victor reached for her.

"Touch me again, Dr. Barrett and you'll be two digits shy of a full hand." She looked at his popcorn box, hoping there was still some in there. "Give me that." She grabbed it and stuffed her hand inside. She felt around to the bottom. *Yes.* There was a handful left. If she had to be at a horror flick, and if she had to sit next to *him*, at least she could eat some buttery popcorn. That counted for something, right?

She crunched down on something hard. Rats. An unpopped kernel? Her tongue went to that side of her mouth. Oh, no. *No no no.* She put her finger in her mouth and came out with something un-popcorn-like. She held up the whatever-it-was towards the light of the screen.

"Noooo!"

More shushing.

Victor scooted closer to her. "What is wrong with you?"

"I uh, nothing."

"Then why did you scream? It's not even a scary part of the movie."

"I…" She didn't want to tell him what happened. If he knew she'd broken a tooth, he, being a dentist, or at least a reasonable facsimile of one, would want to fix it. No way was she letting that man near her mouth. *Except for maybe some more kissing.* Where did that come from? Leave me alone, you traitorous thoughts, you.

"Are you okay?"

"Yeth, I'm fine."

"Did you say 'yeth'?"

Uh-oh. "No. Nope. Huh-uh."

Victor leaned closer and whispered, "Remmie, did you break a tooth on that popcorn?"

She shook her head. "Don't be thilly."

"You did. You broke a tooth. Here, open your mouth and let me see."

She bit his hand.

****

The usher who escorted them out of the theatre was frowning. They were unceremoniously shoved out the door to the sidewalk.

"Well, that went well," said Remmie.

Victor turned toward her. "Say something with an 's' in it."

"What? No."

Victor looked down and pointed. "Look. A snake!"

"Thnake! Where?"

"Ah-ha. I knew it. You broke a tooth."

"All right. Tho what if I did? I'm a dentisth aren't I?"

"You can't fix your own tooth."

"Wanna bet?"

"Don't be absurd. Come on." He grabbed her arm.

"Where are we going?"

"To my office."

Grin & Barrett

"Nooooo."

Three people on the sidewalk shushed them.

****

Victor held her hand as he reached for his keys in his other pocket. "Don't be scared, Remmie, I'm a good dentist."

"But I don't want a Hollywood thmile, Victor."

"I do the regular fix-it stuff too."

"Fith it thuff? Will you be uthing thuperglue?" She tried to pull her hand away from his, but he had tightened his grip.

Victor smirked. "Now that you mention it..."

"What?"

"Kidding." He unlocked the door and pulled her inside.

Remmie gazed around the large waiting room. "Wow."

"You approve?"

What are you doing? If you show your underbelly, he'll attack. "Uh, well, it'th nithe in a pretentiouth thort of way, I gueth."

"Unlike yours, the welcome-to-my-farm look."

"Hey."

"Kidding again." He released her hand. He walked further into the office, turning on light switches as he went. "Come on back Remmie."

She hadn't moved. She didn't want to do this. For one thing, she'd be very close to his lips. And that always got her in trouble. And secondly, she didn't want to owe him anything. If he did this for her, she'd never hear the end of it. It was hard enough just trying to keep him from absconding with her practice.

Victor came back to stand in the doorway to the patient care area. He crooked his finger. "Rem-mie, come on ba-ack."

She sighed. But what choice did she have? Sure, she could wait until Monday and try to get in with one of the other dentists in town, but who knows if they had room in their schedules on such short notice? And, that would mean she'd have to reschedule her own Monday patients. She couldn't afford to make any anyone mad. That would drive them toward Victor all the quicker.

She forced her feet toward the back of the office. She assumed the rest of her body would follow. Although, she wouldn't blame it if it didn't.

Victor was retrieving supplies from a cabinet and setting them on the patient tray. "Have a seat, Remmie." He smiled.

Why was he being so nice all of a sudden? She put her purse on an assistant chair and sat down in the chair he indicated. "I'm thure you won't hurt me, right?"

He raised his eyebrows. "Not on purpose, of course. But you of all people should know the answer to that question. Even when we do our best, sometimes patients have discomfort. I'm sure you get asked it every day in your office, right?"

She nodded. "Juth a little nervouth, I gueth. I'm uthually on the other end of the inthrumenth.

He put on a mask, glasses and gloves. And leaned her back in the chair. Remmie was waiting for some crude comment about how he had her hostage so he could kiss her or have his way with her. Her eyes darted to his.

"Remmie, you're going to be fine, I promise. I really do know what I'm doing."

She nodded and opened her mouth. She squelched an ick as he painted on the topical gel that would ease the discomfort of the needle he would use to numb her. Now she remembered why patients made a face when she used it on them.

"Open wider, please." He moved closer to her.

Good grief her mouth felt like the Grand Canyon as it was. But she opened wide, hoping the hinges of her jaws didn't fly apart.

"There. All done with the injection."

She snapped her mouth shut. All done? She hadn't even felt anything. Man, he was good. Wait. What was she thinking? She could never tell him that.

He slipped off his gloves. "Let me go turn on the stereo while you get numb, okay?" He walked away.

Alone in the room, she looked around at the décor. Not her style. How was he able to get all of this done on such short notice? Probably money. Lots of it. She scooted around trying to get comfortable in the chair. There were gray tile floors. Stainless steel sinks and faucets. Dark blue chairs, lights, and tray tables. Even his mask and gloves were dark blue. Not very cheery. Everything looked cold and unfriendly. Kind of like Victor. Most of the time. He was being kind right now though. And his kisses were anything but cold. Ah! She needed to stop thinking about that. How was she going to make him go away if she kept remembering how wonderful his kisses were? Victor was like candy. You knew it was bad for you, but you couldn't get enough.

He'd put on some soft jazz music. She always played rock. Although, this wasn't bad. She didn't hate it or anything. She lightly bounced her left foot to the tune.

He returned and slipped on a clean pair of gloves. "Are you getting numb?"

She nodded. "Yep."

"Ready for me to begin?"

She shrugged. May as well get it over with. She opened as wide as she could and closed her eyes. She performed this procedure several times a day, every workday, but she knew she was a terrible patient.

"Take deep breaths through your nose, Remmie. It will help you relax."

She inhaled and tried to concentrate on the music. She let out the breath and felt her body go limp.

"Perfect," he said. He hummed along with the background music. Softly. Not in an annoying can't-carry-a-tune way. It was nice. Peaceful. Her eyes stayed closed.

Her silly cats were wearing red top hats and carrying black canes. They whispered behind their paws to each other and pointed at her. What were those two up to now? She looked down at herself. She was wearing a pretty pink dress. Her? A dress? She hadn't seen those legs in a while. They must be hers, though. They were attached to the rest of her.

A noise to her left caught her attention. She turned her head and gasped. Victor had just entered the room. He was wearing a black tuxedo. He looked *scrumptious*. When he held out his hand, she went to him. He twirled her once, then pulled her close. They swayed to the soft romantic music. She laid her cheek on the soft fabric of his jacket lapel. His aftershave was intoxicating. She sighed.

Tap tap tap.

She glanced over her shoulder. Those crazy cats were *tap dancing*. She never should have let them take those dance lessons. But they'd worn her down. They'd told her they wanted to take their act on the road. She'd argued that they couldn't drive themselves without opposable thumbs. And she wasn't selling her dental practice to drive them all over the country to their performances. They hadn't believed her. They said since she was their mom, she'd want to make sure they were happy. And this was their life's dream.

Victor turned her head back toward him with his hand. He caressed her face with his thumbs. See? He had opposable thumbs. And he knew how to use them. She closed her eyes and sighed. His lips brushed over hers. A whisper of a touch. Ah, Victor. So sweet. So loving. She could stay here forever.

"Remmie," he whispered. "I'm all done."

Huh?

"Remmie, I'm all done."

Her eyes popped open. Oh no. She had fallen asleep in Victor's chair. He'd never let her live this down. Had she mumbled something embarrassing in her sleep? Or drooled? Her hand flew to the side of her face but it was numb. It felt like a rubber bicycle tire.

He sat the chair up and removed her patient napkin. Then he took off his gloves, mask and glasses. "You'll be numb for a while, but I'm *sure* you'll be pleased with the result. Because, well, I am the best."

Remmie raised her eyebrows. Oh great. The real Victor was back. Nice Dr. Barrett had left the building. Rats. Bring him back, please. I liked him better.

"Thanth, Victow." She knew her speech still sounded ridiculous, but at least this time it wasn't from a broken tooth. The effects of the anesthesia were temporary.

"You're welcome. See, I told you how good I was." He preened like an over inflated peacock. She could all but see the brilliant blue and green feathers protruding from his back.

He was smirking. Oh, the nerve of that man. When would she learn? She hopped up from the chair, grabbed her purse and stomped out of the office.

Chapter Nine

When Remmie got home, she set her purse on the kitchen table. It took a few seconds of rummaging around in her purse before she found her cell phone. She checked her messages. She'd turned it off in the movie so it wouldn't disturb anyone if it rang. Wouldn't disturb anyone? Between her yelping when Victor blew in her ear at a scary moment in the movie and jumping in his lap, causing soda and popcorn to fly everywhere, she was pretty sure she'd caused a tiny ripple of disturbance. At least the irritated usher told them so.

Another episode she'd never live down. All because of Victor. She'd never had these problems before he came to town. The good-looking scum. She'd always been good-natured Remmie. The girl next door. Dependable. Never getting in trouble. But now? Now she seemed to be in hot water at least once a day. And embarrassed more often than that.

Her phone showed seven messages. All from Carla. Remmie smacked her forehead. *Carla.* The poor girl was probably having a fit trying to figure out where Remmie went and worried sick. She dialed. Carla picked up right away.

"Remmie? Where are you? Are you okay?"

Remmie sighed. "I'm fine."

"Where did you go?"

"Victor and I got evicted from the theatre," she mumbled.

"You got—"

Remmie could tell the phone was covered up on Carla's end. What was that faint noise? Was Carla laughing?

"Hey. Stop that." Remmie heard a swish and figured Carla had removed her hand from over the mouthpiece.

"Sorry. Really. But…evicted?"

"Yep."

"Because…"

"Carla, you were right there. Didn't you notice any unusual noises or movement from my end of the row?"

"Uh, I uh…"

"Oh my gosh. You didn't even notice?" Her voice raised two octaves.

"See, I um—"

"Carla, were you and Joe making out during the movie?"

"I wouldn't say *that*."

"Were you smooching? You *were*. You were smooching. While I was trying to fend off Victor and his ever-grabbing tentacles."

"Sorry, Rem."

Remmie sighed. "It's okay. I guess I don't need to ask if you had a good time."

Carla giggled. "Amazing."

Remmie smiled. "Glad one of us can say that."

"So what happened after you left?"

She tapped her fingers on her table. "Let's say I was introduced to Dr. Barrett in an official capacity."

"What?"

"I broke a tooth on his popcorn."

Carla gasped. "Oh no."

"Oh yes. I didn't see a better alternative at that time of night on a weekend, so I took him up on his offer."

"How did it go?"

"I hate to admit this, but the arrogant jerk has a nice touch. I didn't feel the needle, and the finished product looks and feels great. And..."

"What? Tell me."

"I, uh, fell asleep." She felt her face heat up. But was glad Carla couldn't see it.

"While he was working?"

"Fraid so."

"Oh wow. He *must* be good."

"Don't you dare tell anyone I said that. I'm having a hard enough time holding on to my patients as it is." Remmie's hand tightened on the phone.

"I won't tell a soul. Not even Joe."

Remmie rolled her eyes.

****

The following Monday, Remmie struggled to open the heavy wooden door to the gym. It seemed a person needed to have already worked out just to be able to easily open the door. The smell of chlorine from the attached pool assaulted her nose. The lobby, which was enormous, had pine paneling from floor to ceiling. She located the information desk and marched up to it, determined to get what she wanted.

The woman behind the desk was everything Remmie would never be. Tall. Blonde. Thin. She gave Remmie a look that said, *Why is someone like you even here?*

Remmie tried to ignore the woman's frown. She'd come here for a reason, and she wasn't leaving empty-handed.

"Hello," she said, "I'm Dr. Grin. I'd called earlier about getting some coupons from you to give as incentives to my patients."

The tall woman, whose nametag read, "Kiki" kept frowning. "Well, I wasn't the one who took the call, so I have no idea what you're talking about." She studied her long, manicured fingers, painted blood red.

Remmie realized this wasn't going to go well. Why was the woman being so uncooperative? Wasn't her job to give information? This was the *information desk*, was it not? "Kiki, I spoke to a man. He said his name was Dave. He assured me your gym would be glad to help me out."

"We have three Daves who work here. Which one was it?" Kiki rolled her fake-lashed eyes.

If I knew that, wouldn't I have told you? Remmie plastered a smile on her lips. "He didn't say and I didn't ask. Since I had no idea there would be more than one."

Kiki glared at her. "Wait right here. I'll have to go see which one it was who took your call."

Still forcing a smile, Remmie answered. "Why, thank you. That would be great."

Kiki marched off in stiletto heels that looked about as wide as a toothpick. But then, so was Kiki. Remmie turned around and leaned her back against the marble top of the front counter. Very ritzy place. No wonder she'd never been in here. Not only did she hate to exercise, especially in front of other people, she didn't have the spare cash lying around that she was sure she'd need to belong to a place like this. Male laughter caught her attention to her right. Turning, she could see a large weight room through a sparkling clean picture window. The room appeared to hold at least two dozen workout stations.

Kiki had instructed her to stay right here. But Kiki wasn't the boss of her. Besides, what would it hurt if she innocently ambled over closer to the window? Just for a peek. She sidled in that direction, determined to only stay for a second. Maybe there was a hunk she could feast her eyes on. No harm in that, right? She could look and still not touch.

Every weight bench was occupied by a lifter and a spotter. Most of the men were young. Younger than

Remmie. A few though, seemed more her age or even older. One man, a short, solidly built dark-haired guy, was sitting down to use one of the benches. Very, very handsome. She noticed he wore a wedding ring, though. Not that she was looking or anything. As he lay back to start his repetitions, she spotted the man lying next to him on the adjacent bench. Oh my. Her mouth watered as she took in his hard stomach muscles and bulging biceps. She was grateful the man decided not to wear a shirt. *Thank you very much, Mr. Muscles.* It made it so much easier for her to feast her eyes on his muscular form as he pressed the weights up and down.

As she watched, the man finished and sat up. She gasped. And pressed her hands on the glass. It couldn't be. She'd just drooled over Victor. Victor? She knew he was gorgeous and built, but to see him with him shirt off? Holy smokes! She fanned herself with her hand.

"Excuse me."

Remmie whipped around to find Kiki staring down at her from her stiletto tower. "Oh, uh, did you find the man I was looking for?"

Kiki snickered. "Seems you were doing some looking on your own."

Remmie's hand balled into a tight fist. It would feel so good to smack that skinny, perfect-looking woman into next week. But, she was here for a reason. She needed to play nice. Besides, she didn't have time to get arrested and go to jail.

She rephrased her question. "Were you able to find the man I spoke to *on the phone?*"

Kiki shrugged. "Yes, it was Dave Huggins. He said to give you these." She handed Remmie a stack of coupons with as much enthusiasm as if Remmie had informed her she needed to have her two front teeth painted purple.

"Thank you." Remmie took the coupons, and with what dignity she had left, walked out of the gym.

As soon as she was away from the building, she dug her cell phone out of her purse. Speed-dialing the first number, she waited as it rung once, twice, three and four times. And finally went to voicemail. Where was Carla? She was supposed to be watching the phone at the office. Even though it was the lunch hour, they'd decided for the time being, one of them would be there to answer the phone in case a patient called. Remmie wanted to retain all of her existing patients if at all possible. And out of the clutches of Victor. *Victor.* She still couldn't believe how he'd looked without his shirt. Her breathing sped up at the thought. She wouldn't be able to look him in the eye now without remembering that.

She hurried to her car. If Carla wasn't there, Remmie needed to get to the office and be there to answer the phone. Where would Carla be? This wasn't like her. At all.

When Remmie reached the office, the door was unlocked. She opened it, walked in, and set her purse on the counter. Carla was sitting at the desk. *Hmmm.* Something was up.

"Hey, Remmie, You're back early."

Remmie raised her eyebrows. "You know, it's funny you should mention that, Carla."

"Really?"

Why did her best friend have flushed cheeks? And her hair was messy. Something was *definitely* up. "I tried calling here about ten minutes ago. But you didn't pick up."

"Really? Hmmm. Gosh. Not sure what could have happened."

Remmie put her hands on her hips. "Carla? What is going on?"

Her friend blushed. "Please don't be mad, Remmie. Joe dropped by. He...we....it kind of got out of hand. We started kissing, and I guess I didn't even hear the phone ring."

Carla was happy. That was obvious. How could Remmie be upset?

"It's okay, Car. I'm not mad. Just, maybe in the future, do your smooching outside of work?"

Carla smiled. "Sure. Not a problem. And I am sorry."

They hugged. Remmie was glad they had such a close friendship. They could never stay mad at each other for long.

"So why were you calling?"

"Hmmm?"

"You said you tried calling here."

Remmie's face felt hot. "Uh..."

"Why are you blushing? The last time was because you'd met...Victor. This has something to do with him, doesn't it?"

"Yes. Definitely."

"Spill it sister."

Remmie leaned on the counter. "I went down to the gym to get those coupons they promised. Their snippy receptionist didn't know anything about them so she left to go find out. While she was gone I happened to see—"

"Victor was there?"

Remmie nodded. "Oh boy was he. He was...Carla, the man was lifting weights. Without a shirt. He looked good. And I do mean *good*."

"Ah. That explains the blush. But I thought you didn't like him, Rem."

"That's the crazy thing. Most of the time I'd like to smack him upside his perfect hair-do. But, when he looks at me, or touches me, or especially kisses me. I just...." Remmie shrugged.

"Lose control?"
"You got it."
"Believe me, I know."

Remmie smiled. At least they understood each other well enough to confide in each other, knowing it would go no further.

Chapter Ten

Victor went over his work schedule for the day. Three of the patients were from Remmie's office. When he'd first met her, that wouldn't have bothered him as much. Especially with his uncle keeping a tight fist on the purse strings. But, the more he got to know her, and the more he kissed her, it bothered him. A lot. If only there was another way around this. But Victor was caught between a demanding, unmovable uncle, and a woman he'd come to care about. Very much. Remmie would have a fit when she learned of these three latest patients. He couldn't blame her. Why couldn't the woman just accept his offer? It would make all of these problems go away. Then maybe they could stop fighting all the time. And get to know each other better.

He picked up the stack of charts his assistant had left on his desk. With what his uncle was proposing, Remmie would have it made. She could stay and work for Victor, or start a new practice in another location. Her choice. Either way, she'd be a lot better off financially than she ever could be on her own. She was so stubborn. She wasn't backing down. He frowned. Well, neither was he. If he didn't come through on this for Tobias, he'd be disowned. And stuck with a hefty bill to pay back. Tobias was already leaving him frequent messages, asking what was taking so long. Victor didn't know what to tell him. He wasn't ready to admit defeat. There had to be a way.

He walked to the front door of his office. Was that Remmie outside on the sidewalk? He watched her through the window. What was she doing? It looked as if

Grin & Barrett

she was handing out pieces of paper to people walking by. Hmmm. This didn't look good. What was she up to? Someone stopped in front of Victor's window. They had the paper turned so he could see it. It was a coupon to a gym. His gym. He recognized the logo. Was she trying to entice patients to come to her office with those?

And why didn't he ever receive the box of gifts he ordered? It reminded him then what he was doing. The same thing Remmie was doing. Trying to buy patients. But, he had to do what was necessary. He rubbed the back of his neck. And Remmie just made it a whole lot harder.

****

Remmie watched Victor leave at lunchtime. Where was he going? He almost never left for lunch. She sat at her counter beside her front window. When he returned a half-hour later, he unrolled a poster-sized photo of himself and hung it on the outside of his window. Right out on the sidewalk where everyone could see it. She couldn't let him get away with that.

She went outside a few minutes later to see it up close. Victor was standing in front of it.

Remmie snorted. "What-cha got there, Doc? A Wanted Poster?"

She laughed until two young women stopped to admire the picture. They smiled at Victor when they realized he was the man in the photo. After asking Victor if he was taking new patients, they followed him into his front office door.

Remmie stood on the sidewalk with her mouth hanging open. That did not just happen. *Well, we'll just see about that!*

****

The following morning, Remmie hung her own professionally made photo poster in her front window. She'd just see who got more patients with their pictures.

Victor came outside to stand by her on the sidewalk. "Nice picture, Remmie."

"Thank you, Dr. Barrett."

"I thought we dropped the doctor, since there was all the kissing."

Remmie glared at him. "Read my lips, Dr. Barrett. There will be no more kissing."

"Really? Well that's a shame. I thought we did it quite well together."

He grabbed her and pulled her toward him. Placing his lips on hers, he bent her back in an old-fashioned dip. When he brought her back up, he released her. Saluted the small group of people who had gathered to point and stare, and waltzed into his office.

Remmie, wiping Victor's kiss from her lips with the back of her hand, hurried into her office as well.

Of all the nerve of that man. How dare he kiss her right out on a busy sidewalk? And right after she'd told him in no uncertain terms that there would be no more kissing? This was war.

That evening, Remmie waited until it was dark and she knew Victor had left for the day. She waited around her office after everyone had gone home. She snuck out of her front door with her flashlight and black magic marker. A budding artist was about to make her debut.

****

Remmie's first patient came in. It was a teenage boy she'd had as a patient since he was eight.

"Hey, Todd, how are you?" Remmie smiled at him.

"I'm good, Dr. Grin. Better than you, though, I guess."

Her smile faded. "What do you mean?"

He laughed and pointed toward the front window, where several neighborhood business people were staring at her photo and chuckling.

Rushing out the door, she skidded to a stop in front of her window. There, on her photo were some accessories she hadn't originally included.

"Hey doc," said Orville Conley, the baker from two doors down. "Nice buck teeth."

"And don't forget the ears. Gotta love those," said Candy Wright, the secretary at the bank.

"But the best thing, I think, is the words coming out of the mouth."

Remmie turned toward the third speaker. Victor. Who, of course, was smirking. The nerve of that man. Where her lovely picture had been was now a buck-toothed donkey, saying the words "Don't be a jackass. Go see the best dentist in town: Dr. Victor Barrett."

Laughing, the group floated away to start their own workdays. Remmie balled up her fists and faced Victor.

"How dare you."

He raised his eyebrow. "Excuse me?"

"You defaced my picture." She ripped hers down from the window.

"You defaced mine first." He ripped his down, too. "The beard and glasses weren't bad, but the blackened teeth got under my skin."

"I did it because you kissed me."

"And that was because you told me I couldn't. You don't seem to understand who you're dealing with, Remmie. I will not give up until I get what I want."

"Oh yeah? Well neither will I."

They both retreated to their offices. The two office doors slammed in unison.

Remmie stormed into her office. Todd glanced up at her from the waiting room chair. He looked a little frightened. Remmie realized she couldn't let this get to her. Not when she had a job to do. She smiled at Todd.

"Thanks for telling me about that." She pointed to the window. "Ready for your filling?"

Todd shrugged. "As ready as a person could ever be to be poked at, drilled on, and numb for half his life."

Remmie laughed and led him to the back of the office. "Why Todd, I think you'd make a wonderful dentist some day."

He groaned. But Remmie noticed he seemed awfully interested in whatever Darcy was doing. Maybe that's why he never missed his appointments?

Remmie had two phone calls that day from patients who had received her coupon from the gym. They asked questions about her services and prices, but didn't make appointments. She'd bet anything they would go to Victor because of his ad in the paper about half-priced initial services. She sighed. To compete with Victor, she was going to have to do the same thing. She couldn't afford to. But she couldn't afford not to, either. And even though it pained her to do it, she knew she had to return the box of gifts Victor had ordered back to him. She'd do everything she could to not sell her practice. But she would not steal.

She taped up Victor's box and scooted it with her hip towards the door. It took her three tries to hoist the box over the threshold. More scooting got it in front of Victor's office door. He could take it from there. He couldn't miss it. It was big enough to house a moose.

****

Victor picked up yet another bill to be forwarded to his uncle. He had a dilemma. A big one. How was he going to explain to his uncle that he still hadn't got Remmie to sell to them? Uncle Tobias was unbending. Victor had never known him to be otherwise. And it seemed the older his uncle got, the worse he became.

And Remmie was stubborn. Victor understood her reasons for not wanting to sell. He really did. But couldn't she see how much better off she'd be financially if she took the generous offer? She wouldn't even listen to reason. He sighed. But wasn't that one thing he admired about her? She stood up for what she wanted. What she believed in. That was more than Victor was willing to do. Yes, he agreed that Remmie would have more money if she accepted, but would she be happier?

Victor tapped the end of his pen on the desk. He wished he didn't have to rely on his uncle's money. Then Tobias would leave him alone. He could no longer call the shots in Victor's life. If Victor was strong like Remmie, he'd just walk away. But he was scared. Of what the future would hold. Of struggling. Ever since his uncle had moved in with his mom and him, they'd no longer had to scratch to make ends meet. He'd gotten used to having plenty of money. He wasn't sure he remembered how to live any other way. He'd also feel like a failure if he had to fight just to stay afloat. He stood up from the desk and walked toward the back of the office. But, did he consider Remmie a failure? No. Not in the least. She was admirable, strong, and competent. So why couldn't he see himself the same way if he stopped counting on his uncle?

****

Remmie hurried to answer her doorbell. Swinging open the heavy oak door, the smile she had on her face for the prospective visitor was replaced by a frown.

"Good Morning, Remmie." Victor grinned at her.

"Hello, Dr. Barrett."

"As many times as you've kissed me, don't you think we could drop the doctor?"

She'd like to drop this doctor. Maybe off a cliff. She sighed. "What can I do for you?"

He looked down. "You're not wearing any shoes."

"I don't wear them at home. I like going barefooted."

"Well, you need to put on your shoes and come with me."

She raised both eyebrows. "And I would do this because…"

"I signed us up for some jail time."

"Excuse me?"

Victor crossed his arms. "You know, you're put in a fake jail, then you call people and have them pay fake bail. The money goes toward the school system."

"I know what it is, Victor. What makes you think I'll sit in jail with you?"

"The mayor wants the city's professionals to pair up. Dentists, Doctors, Teachers. Come on, it will be fun."

"Do I have to do this? I mean I wouldn't mind doing it at another time. With someone else, but, I'd rather not be cooped up—"

"With me?"

"Well…" She looked away.

"We're signed up for a certain time slot. Ours starts in fifteen minutes."

Remmie put her hands on her jeans-covered hips, as she turned her head back toward him. "And why am I just now finding out about this?"

"Because you would have said no."

"You're right about that." She frowned. "But I guess I don't have an excuse good enough to get out of this. Let me get my shoes and purse."

When she came back downstairs, Victor had let himself in. She hadn't invited him because once he was in her vicinity, things seemed to happen. Embarrassing things. Victor sat on her brown leather couch, looking quite pleased with himself. And too comfortable.

Remmie's cats had followed her down the stairs. They both stopped in their tracks when they saw Victor. Winston kept his distance, crouching and sniffing the air a few feet from the intruder, his tail lashing. But Charles trotted into the living room and sidled up to Victor's leg. The cat rubbed his face against the man's shin.

"Remmie, what's he—"

Charles leaped in the air and onto Victor's lap. Victor's eyes grew large.

Remmie giggled. "Victor, you remember Charles and Winston. Seems Winston remembers your kiss and doesn't want a repeat. Charles, though, he seems to have taken a shine to you."

Victor sat still. Not a muscle twitched. His eyes were fixed on the cat, who turned in a circle and cuddled up for a catnap, curling his long tail around his body. And purred.

"Not now, Charles, we're leaving." She scooped up her cat, placing him on a nearby chair. The cat narrowed his eyes and harrumphed at her.

Victor popped up as if the couch was on fire. "Thank you. That was horrible."

Remmie shook her head. "No it wasn't. Don't be ridiculous. Come on. Let's get the torture over with."

He pointed back at the couch. "Oh, I don't see how it could be any worse than that."

****

The 'jail' was a small wooden shed with several windows. Inside were a couch, a chair, and a lamp.

Remmie put down her purse, "What, no TV? No snacks?"

Victor frowned.

"I'm kidding."

"Remmie, this is a very important cause."

"I know that." She sat down in the chair.

Victor sat on the couch. "Why don't you make yourself comfortable over here?" He patted the cushion next to him.

"No thanks. This chair is fine."

"Oh, come on. You know you want to."

"No, I really don't."

"All right. If you won't sit on the couch with me, we'll share the chair you're sitting on."

Remmie jumped up. There was no way she was sharing the chair with him. That would mean she'd be on his lap. *Huh-uh.*

She sat on the end of the couch, as far away as she could get. Victor scooted closer until he was right beside her.

"Victor, you're crowding me."

"I know." He smiled.

"Scoot over." She shoved at his shoulder. He didn't budge. She remembered how he'd looked without his shirt at the gym. She felt her face grow hot.

"Why are you blushing?"

"No reason. N-nothing. Hey, aren't we supposed to be calling people to rescue us?"

"Yes. We are." He took out his cell phone and dialed.

"Who are you calling?"

"My lab guy, Dan. But he's not answering." He left a message. "Okay your turn."

Remmie took her phone out of her purse and dialed Carla. It rang and rang. Voicemail. "Guess I have to leave a message too."

Victor tried a couple of other people, but since he was new to town, he didn't know that many people yet. Remmie left a few messages with Darcy and different friends. Where was everyone?

Victor put his arm on the back of the couch behind her. "Guess we're stuck here for the full three hours unless someone bails us out."

"Yep. Guess so." Good grief. She was stuck in this little wooden house for three hours. With Victor. And his lips.

She needed to keep him talking. That seemed to be the only way he wasn't using his lips for kissing.

"So," she said, "what happens if no one bails us out? The cause won't get any money?"

He shook his head. "No, they'll get money. It will come from us."

"Oh. Well, that's good. I'd hate for the three hours to have been a waste of time."

"Oh, they won't. Trust me."

Her mouth dropped open. "Trust you?"

He smiled the smile she was coming to know so well. The one that both infuriated and captivated her. How did he do that? She was a pretty determined, strong-willed person. How was it that as soon as he was in her personal space, she lost all sense of reason?

She turned her face away from him. "So, I guess since we're here together, we could, um, talk."

"Sure. Talk away."

She turned back toward him. "Oh. I was hoping you would talk." She needed to keep those lips busy.

"About what?"

"Anything." *Please just start talking.*

He shrugged. "Uh, okay. I've already told you about my Uncle Tobias."

"The one holding your puppet strings."

He glared at her. "No, it's not like that."

"Sure sounds like it to me." She tapped her index finger on the arm of the couch.

"You've got it all wrong."

"Enlighten me."

He removed his arm from the back of the couch. He leaned forward so his forearms were on his knees. "My dad left my mom and me when I was thirteen. Uncle Tobias is her younger brother. Much younger He's only seventeen years older than me. He moved in with us, to help my mom out around the house."

Remmie nodded. Encouraging him to continue.

"He was thirty years old then. He'd been out of dental school for only four years, but his practice was already substantial. He has a knack for business. He was able to buy out an existing practice of another dentist who was retiring. He's done very well for himself. He encouraged me to go to dental school too, when the time came. And, against my mom's protests, he paid my entire bill. Everything."

"Victor, I'm sorry your dad left. That's awful. And I'm glad you and your mom have your uncle. But I still don't see how that makes it okay to try to pressure other dentists, like me, to sell to you."

"My uncle is a very smart man. He sees business trends before most people would ever even think to look. My whole career has been because of his generosity so...."

She tilted her head towards him. "So when he said he wanted you to buy me out, and have one huge office where there would have been two, you did it. No questions asked."

Victor said nothing.

Remmie put her hand on his arm. "Victor. Don't you see how wrong this is?"

"But we're prepared to offer you a very good price. And, I'd want you to stay on and work for me. Remmie I know you probably don't have a lot of extra money lying around. This would help you out."

"Don't try to sound as if you were doing me a favor."

"That's exactly what I'm saying."

She lowered her eyebrows. "Victor, my practice means everything to me. You have no idea how hard I've worked. My whole family told me it was a bad idea. That I'd never make it on my own. But, I have. No, it hasn't been easy. Ever. But I'm still here. And I will continue to be here. You don't understand how important it is to me to have my own practice."

"And you don't understand how important it is to me for you to sell it to me."

She sighed. "I guess that leaves us back at square one."

"Yes, I guess it does."

Remmie removed her hand from Victor's arm, prepared to go back to the chair. Victor placed his hand over hers. Stopping her from leaving. She turned to look at him. What did she see in his eyes. Regret? Sadness?

Victor placed his other hand under her chin, rubbing his thumb against her cheek. She closed her eyes. She inhaled his spicy aftershave. And sighed. When his lips touched hers, her only thought was, why can't it always be like this? Why do we have to have this problem between us?

He pulled her closer. Somehow she ended up sitting on his lap. Right where she hadn't wanted to end up if they'd been in the chair. But right now, that didn't seem to matter. All that mattered was his arms around her, holding her tight. Making her feel warm and loved. He held her like that for what seemed an eternity. But not nearly long enough.

The knock on the door startled them. Remmie climbed off of Victor's lap and stood up, smoothing down her rumpled shirt

The door creaked opened. It was Carla and Joe. "You're rescued, Rem. We bailed you out." She gasped. "Oh, you're not alone."

Victor remained seated on the couch while Remmie stood, blocking Carla's view at first.

"No," said Remmie, "we, um, decided to do this together."

Carla raised her eyebrows and smiled. "Okay, then. Anybody up for some pizza?"

Chapter Eleven

Remmie sat next to Victor in their booth at the pizza place. She couldn't believe how nice he was being. Why couldn't he be like this all the time? She'd only seen him be a troll with her. For some reason she brought out the worst in him. Maybe that had something to do with the giant hippo in the room. He wanted her to sell her practice. She lowered her eyebrows. She didn't want to. There didn't seem to be any middle ground. But here at the pizza place, with her and Carla and Joe, he seemed...sweet. Funny. Loveable even. She watched as Joe and Victor tried to outdo each other seeing how many large salad croutons they could eat at once. Crunch. Crunch. He was being *goofy*. Like a normal *guy*.

Carla couldn't stop laughing. Then Remmie laughed. She could never stay serious when Carla started snorting. Then she snorted. They sounded like a couple of baby pigs.

When their dinner was finished, Joe and Carla left to spend some time alone. Which left, of course, Remmie alone with Victor. Would he revert back to his old annoying self? He surprised her by paying for her dinner. She shook her head. Would wonders never cease?

They walked back to Victor's car. Until today, Remmie hadn't been in it since the night they had dinner together that first time. When she was drippy from the rain. And mad. And he kissed her, saying he loved a challenge. Hmmm. Comparing the rest of it with that kiss, it didn't seem like such an awful night somehow. And the way he was looking at her right that moment told her he wanted a repeat. Now.

This time Remmie knew it was coming. This time she didn't argue. She leaned toward him and wrapped her arms around his neck, pulling his lips toward hers. Her hands fell to his shoulders. The softness of his lips and the hardness of his shoulder muscles sent her senses spiraling. She felt as if she'd always known him. But also as if he was the one she'd been searching for.

As Victor took a step back, he positioned himself firmly against the side of his car. He pulled her close, whispering her name, kissing her lips, cheeks, and neck. Rubbing his lips across her earlobe. Remmie sighed. Why couldn't they always be like this? Why did they have to fight?

He drove her home, holding her hand the whole way. She looked down at their entwined fingers. How could he keep her senses on overload, just by rubbing her hand with his thumb? Victor pulled into her driveway. After they climbed the front steps and Remmie had unlocked the door, she invited him in. When they reached her living room, they kept on kissing. Where had this man been all her life? She tugged on his hand.

"Come over here. Let's sit on the couch."

He followed her, taking her in his arms as soon as they were seated. She sighed and closed her eyes, waiting for his lips to touch hers again. Something soft touched Remmie's arm. She opened her eyes and looked down.

"Oh, hi Charles," she said.

Victor stiffened.

Remmie laughed. "Victor, if we're going to be together, you've got to get over this *whatever it is* with animals. Charles and Winston are my family."

Victor frowned. "What would I have to do?"

"Well, for starters, you could pet one of them. Charles seems to like you. Although, I don't think poor Winston has ever gotten over that kiss at the vet's office."

Victor scowled. "I'm not sure I'm over it either."

"Here." she picked up Charles and set him on Victor's lap.

"What now?"

She took his hand and laid it on the cat's soft back. "Just pet him."

Victor tentatively touched the cat. Charles purred.

Victor looked at Remmie. "What's he doing?"

"Purring. Remember that day at the vet's office? You heard them purring and didn't like it."

He frowned. "Well, maybe it's not as repulsive as I thought at first."

"There ya go."

"There I go, what?"

"You're giving it the old college try."

He looked at her. "I've always wondered. What old college is it, and why were they always trying?"

She smacked his chest. "You're avoiding your responsibility."

"I am?"

"Yes. Pet the cat."

He tried again. This time with longer strokes. Charles hunkered down on Victor's lap and kneaded his paws. Victor's eye opened wide. "I think I made him mad."

"No, that's a good thing. They do that when they're happy. The kneading is something they did as kittens. With their mothers."

He stopped stroking the cat's fur. "Are you trying to tell me this cat thinks I'm his mother?"

Remmie tried to hold back her laugh with her hand. It didn't work. "Victor, no…I, I'm…" More laughing. "It reminds him of a happier time. He doesn't think you're *her*."

"Maybe I'm not doing this right. Maybe you'd better take him back."

Winston jumped up on Remmie's lap and crouched down for a nap. She shrugged and smiled at Victor. "Hmmm. Sorry. Looks like the no vacancy sign on my lap just went up. You're going to have to hold him for a while."

He sighed. "If I must."

"You must."

"Wow, you sure ask a lot of a guy."

"Oh. Victor, we're just getting started.

****

Victor had dropped Remmie off at her house a half hour before. He still sat in his car in his driveway. Soft jazz played on the radio. What was he going to do? Tobias was closing in, pestering him more and more. Now his calls were daily. But Victor was no closer to getting Remmie to sell her practice than he was that first day they'd met. He ran his hand over his eyes. He'd tried telling his uncle that Remmie wouldn't budge. That she had no desire to sell or work for someone else. But Tobias hadn't accepted that. He said everyone had a price. And it was up to Victor to find out what it was and get her practice.

The more Victor bugged Remmie about it, the more she refused. And the more she refused, the less Victor wanted to bug her. He shook his head. He didn't like seeing her upset. He was falling for her. Hard. He wanted Remmie to be happy. And if that was her keeping her own practice, then that's what he wanted, too. There had to be a way to please both of them. He just couldn't for the life of him figure out what that would be. He needed more time to come up with a plan.

He was being pulled in both directions. Uncle Tobias, because he owed him so much, and Remmie, because he...loved her. How could he resolve this? He turned off the ignition, got out of the car, and walked to his front door.

Once inside his house, he made a decision. He wasn't sure yet how he would convince his uncle to back off, but he'd come up with something. Given enough time. Right now, the important thing was to make sure Remmie knew he was done badgering her. About the practice. He wasn't planning on leaving her alone on a personal level at all. This was only beginning. He had wonderful plans for her on that score.

****

Remmie's cell phone rang. It was Victor.

"Hi Victor. Um, you've only been gone for like thirty minutes. Everything okay?"

"Yeah. Everything's great."

She laughed. "Wow, usually I don't get such a positive response from you. Just the opposite in fact."

Victor was silent.

Remmie frowned. "What's up?"

"Remmie, you don't need to worry about me bugging you to sell your practice anymore."

"I don't?" Her mouth dropped open. Was he serious?

"No. It's taken care of."

"Just like that?"

"Yep. Now maybe you and I can concentrate on more pleasant things."

Remmie smiled. Who was this nice, non-confrontational man on the phone? "Victor, I'd like that very much. Thanks for…well, thanks."

"Good-night, Remmie. Sleep well."

He hung up.

Remmie sighed as she hung up, too. She knew she'd sleep better tonight than she had in weeks. After brushing her teeth, she headed to bed. She usually read for a while, but didn't feel the need tonight. She closed her eyes, taking a deep breath as she relaxed into the pillow.

Her dream was the same one she'd had before. Only before, the man was someone she didn't know. Just a man stuck in her dream, holding a spot open for her true love to come. But this time, the man was Victor. Tall, muscular, blue-eyed Victor. They held hands as they walked down toward the stream. Remmie had packed a picnic basket with all their favorite foods. Spreading the red and white checked tablecloth in the ground beside them, Victor set out the food. But, there was something else in the basket. What was it? She reached her hand in.

"No, let me," said Victor.

Remmie nodded. What could it be?

He lifted out a small gift bag. Reaching into the bag, he produced a tiny, red velvet hinged box.

Remmie gasped. Could it be? She looked into Victor's eyes. He smiled. The smile she'd come to adore. He opened the box. Inside, was a beautiful, sparkling diamond set in gold, with tiny garnets surrounding the larger stone.

"Oh, Victor."

He removed the ring and reached for her hand. Placing the ring on her finger, he kissed the back of her fingers.

"It's lovely, Victor."

"Like you."

She looked at him. Waiting for the question. Although they both knew what she'd say.

"Remmie Grin, will you marry me?"

"Was there any doubt?"

He threw back his head and laughed. "Maybe at first. But not now. Never again."

The kiss was sweet and seductive, all at once.

****

Remmie sat at her front counter the next Monday, going over her charts. A never-ending job. Small price to pay for having her own business, though. And now that

Victor wasn't pressuring her to sell anymore, she could relax. And, her relationship with Victor could grow to reach a new level. She'd waited her whole life for Victor. She just didn't realize it until now. He was competitive, arrogant, fussy and picky. But, she loved him. Yes, she knew it to be true. She was in love with Victor Barrett. And she felt certain he was in love with her.

The front door opened. Remmie glanced up from her charts. She wasn't expecting any more patients today. Maybe someone new, wanted to make an appointment? She'd take all she could get. The man was older, maybe sixty, short and bald. Hmmm. Wasn't that how Victor had described his uncle?

She stood up. "Hello, may I help you?"

"Hello, Dr. Remmie Grin?"

"Yes, I'm Dr. Grin."

The man walked to her counter and stuck out his hand. "I'm Dr. Tobias Shultz."

Remmie smiled and shook his hand. "Victor's uncle. How nice to meet you."

He smiled. "And you as well. May we talk for a few minutes?"

Remmie wasn't sure what they'd have to talk about. She'd be surprised if Victor had confided in his uncle about his relationship with her given the tumultuous relationship between the two men.

"Sure," she said, "let's sit down over here." She led him to her waiting room chairs and indicated he should sit. She sat down in the chair next to him, folded her hands in her lap and waited.

Dr. Shultz turned in his seat to face her. "May I call you Remmie?"

She smiled. "Yes, of course."

"Remmie, I'm so pleased with how things are going."

So, Victor must have confided in his uncle after all?
"Um, thank you. So am I."

"At first I didn't think things would work out."

"Neither did I."

"Victor would keep me updated. I'd call to check up on him every couple of days or so."

Remmie lowered her eyebrows. Victor must have understated how he got along with Tobias. She had the impression they weren't close at all. Maybe she'd misunderstood. Or something had drastically changed.

"I'd like for you and Victor to join me for dinner this evening. My treat."

Remmie smiled. "Thank you. That would be lovely."

"Splendid. I'll pick the two of you up here at seven. Does that work for you?"

"Yes. Thanks." She remembered that was the exact scenario of her first date with Victor. She certainly hoped tonight had a better outcome. Although, she and Victor had worked things out since then. Thank goodness.

As soon as Tobias had left, Remmie went outside and walked to Victor's office door. She peeked in the window. A woman sat reading a magazine in the waiting room. Victor didn't run behind much, so the woman probably wasn't waiting to be seen herself. This late in the afternoon, he should be about finished. Maybe the woman was waiting on whoever the patient was in the back. A child, perhaps? That would mean Victor was on his last patient, was already in the midst of the procedure, and wouldn't be much longer. She wanted to talk to him before dinner, but needed to go home and shower and change.

As she drove home, she realized she was excited to get to know someone from Victor's family. It hadn't seemed important up till now. Victor hadn't met hers yet, either, but now that they were getting more serious, he'd surely be meeting them soon. Even though she didn't have a close relationship with them, unfortunately. But they weren't like her. They cared about money. And power. And they never believed in her. That kind of sounded like Victor when she first met him. Not now, though. He had changed.

After her shower, she changed into the same outfit she'd worn that first night with Victor. She hadn't had a chance to go clothes shopping since that night. This dinner was bringing up a lot of not so pleasant memories. She shrugged them off as she got ready for her…what? It wasn't actually a date. Not with Uncle Tobias there. Oh, well, it didn't matter what she called it. Fastening her earrings and necklace, she faced the reflection in the mirror. She was determined to enjoy herself getting to know Victor's uncle. Maybe he'd even tell some old family stories about Victor she could use as blackmail later. She laughed.

Her cats once again desperately wanted to help her get ready.

"Come on, guys. It's the same thing as last time. I need to make a good impression. This time on Victor's uncle. So, as much as I love you, and adore holding and petting you, you can't help me get ready. Not this time, okay?" She laughed when they seemed to be frowning at her. Displeased by her instructions.

****

She stood outside her office. Waiting. And checked her watch again. She thought Victor would be here by now. She'd left him a couple of voicemails to call her but he'd never returned them. Which was odd, considering how he'd bugged her so much when they'd first met, and wouldn't leave her alone. Maybe he was at home getting ready, too, and didn't have to time check his phone.

A black Mercedes pulled up to the curb. The driver's side door opened and Tobias got out.

"Hello, Remmie, don't you look lovely."

"Why thank you. Um," She pointed towards Victor's office. "Victor isn't here yet."

Tobias frowned. "We have reservations. Why don't you and I go ahead and he can meet us there? I'll leave him a message to do just that." Remmie didn't like the idea of going ahead without Victor, but didn't see where she had a choice. His uncle seemed a power to be reckoned with. He reminded her a lot of the men in her family. But then, so had Victor. At first.

They pulled up in front of Fond Memories. Again. How much déjà vu could a girl take? She waited as Tobias came around to let her out of the passenger side door. He reached down to take her hand and help her up onto the sidewalk. Once inside, her eyes darted around the room. Maybe Victor was already here? She still hadn't spotted him as they were led to a table near the back. At least it wasn't the same table. They were seated, and a waiter asked for their drink orders.

Remmie leaned toward Tobias. "Shouldn't we wait for Victor?"

He waived his hand in her direction. "He'll be along. I left him a message to meet me here. He'll show up."

Remmie nodded and shrugged, as she picked up a menu. She was determined this time to order for herself. And get something she liked to eat. Nothing icky for her tonight.

"So sorry I'm late, Uncle Tobias."

"See that it doesn't happen again, Victor."

Remmie looked up at Victor. He seemed startled. But why would he be?

"Remmie," he said, "I didn't expect you to be here." His face turned red. Was that a sheen of sweat on his forehead?

She frowned. "Your uncle invited me. Is…something wrong?"

"No. No, of course not." He sat down hard on his chair, almost losing his balance. What was wrong with him?

The waiter scooted up to their table. "Are you ready to order, sir?" He looked only at Tobias.

"Yes, I'll have the sirloin tips, rare, Caesar salad, and baked squash."

Remmie's eyes widened. Amazing. The man and his nephew really were a lot alike. She was thankful, though, when the waiter approached her next and took her order. At least she would be able to enjoy her food. Victor ordered, absently-mindedly it seemed, as if he didn't even give it thought. He ordered what Remmie ordered. How odd. Didn't he even pay attention to what she'd said? That wasn't like him. He was ordinarily precise and decisive.

Tobias folded his hands in front of him on the table. "Victor, I was telling Remmie earlier how pleased I am with how things have turned out."

Victor looked as if he was going to be ill. His face was now pale. His breathing shallow.

"I'm very much looking forward to moving ahead with our plans," continued his uncle.

Remmie looked at Tobias. What plans was he talking about? Did he have more in mind for Victor's practice? She looked at Victor and smiled. Surely he would be excited about good news for his dental office. His eyes darted toward her, then looked away. Why was he sweating? It wasn't at all hot in the room. In fact, Remmie was a little chilly. Should she be worried? Was he okay?

Tobias was waxing poetic about the quaintness of Remmie's little town when their food arrived. Remmie was thrilled she'd at least gotten to choose what she wanted to eat. She'd never let someone else order for her again.

Victor looked down at his food and frowned. He tilted his head to the side, as if trying to figure out how in the world he'd ended up with something so repulsive. *Well, join the club Victor*, she thought, *it ain't so much fun to be stuck with something you don't like, is it?*

Tobias squinted his eyes and looked at Victor's plate. "What on earth are you eating, son?"

Victor didn't speak. Simply shrugged, as if even that took all his energy. Remmie was getting even more concerned. Maybe Victor was coming down with something. Did he have a fever? Is that why he was sweating?

Tobias shook his head. "No matter. The whole reason we're here is to celebrate."

Remmie raised her eyebrows. My goodness, the man certainly took someone else's relationship seriously. Maybe he'd never been romantically involved with anyone, and was living vicariously.

He looked at Victor and Remmie and raised his glass. "Here's to many, many years of Dr. Grin working with us. We're so glad to have you come under our dental umbrella." *What?* Remmie whipped her head toward Victor. His eyes held a pleading look now. "Victor?"

He just shook his head.

"What is going on? What is your uncle talking about?" Her heartbeat sped up. This couldn't be happening. It was a joke, right?

Victor held his hand out toward her. "Remmie, I...I'm so sorry. I wanted to tell you, but—"

"See here," said Tobias, "what's all this about? Victor, you told me she was in."

"In what?" Her hands balled into fists. She refused to take Victor's hand. What was going on?

"Why, in with us, Remmie. That you'd sold your practice to us."

Remmie's mouth hung open. "Excuse me?"

Tobias glared at his nephew. "Victor. You led me to believe everything was taken care of. You've got some explaining to do."

Remmie glared at him, too. "Yes, you certainly do." She was shaking. She couldn't stop. She'd never felt this angry.

Victor shook his head slowly. "I'm sorry. To both of you. I was caught in the middle, trying to please everyone."

Tobias threw his white cloth napkin down on the table. "Well, son, that simply won't do." He stood up abruptly and stormed out of the restaurant. Remmie had the fleeting thought that she'd done the same thing just a few weeks ago. She turned toward Victor. The man she'd come to love. The man she'd come to trust.

"Victor? How could you lie to me? I thought we were past that. I thought we were getting closer." Her heart was beating so fast and hard. Would it pound right out of her chest? Her breathing was coming in short gasps. How could this be happening? Just when they were getting along?

He reached for her hand. "Remmie, I'm so sorry. I never meant to lie to you or hurt you in any way. Please believe me. I'd hoped to talk Tobias out of pushing for you to sell to us before you ever found out. Please forgive me. I care about you so much."

She pulled her hand away from him. "You've got a terrible way of showing it. I trusted you." She followed Tobias' example and left Victor sitting at the table. Alone.

This time when she walked home from the restaurant, at least it wasn't raining. Her feet felt as heavy as boat anchors. And her chest hurt. She was either having a heart attack, or her heart was breaking. Why? Why was this happening? She forced her feet to keep moving. She had to get away from here. Away from Victor.

Victor cruised up beside her in his car. "Remmie, please listen to me."

She kept on walking, trying to ignore his very existence. Her tears were making it difficult to see the sidewalk clearly. She hoped she wouldn't trip. Wouldn't that be lovely right now? Broken bones and a broken heart, all at once.

"Remmie, please."

She glared at him. "Go away, Victor. I thought you had changed. But obviously I was wrong."

"No, you were right. Please, stop so we can talk."

She turned away from him and kept walking. She heard brakes, a car door slam. Steps running behind her. Victor was now beside her, grabbing her hand.

"Please stop walking."

She was so furious with him, she was shaking. "Victor. I trusted you. And I thought I—"

"You what?"

"Never mind."

"What, Remmie?"

Her gaze went to the sidewalk. "I thought I was falling in love with you."

"Oh Remmie."

"Don't *oh Remmie* me. You're a traitor and a louse."

He gave her a watery smile. "At least I'm no longer a snake."

She knew what he was doing. He was trying to make her laugh. It wasn't going to work. "Go home, Victor. I don't want to talk to you."

"But Remmie—"

She turned toward him, hands planted on her hips. "Listen closely. I do not want to talk to you. I do not want to see you. Go away and leave me alone. Clear enough for you?"

Chapter Twelve

The gifts arrived early the next morning. If the deliveryman brought in many more, Remmie would have to seat her patients out on the sidewalk. What was she supposed to do with all of it?

"Remmie," said Carla. "What is going on?"

Remmie heaved a sigh, trying not to cry. "Oh Carla, last night…"

"What?"

"You know I had dinner with Victor and his uncle?" Remmie crossed her arms over her chest.

"Right."

"It didn't turn out so great."

Carla pointed toward the phone. "Listen, our first patient just called and canceled. Her son has the flu. We have time to sit down and talk." She took Remmie's hand and maneuvered around two huge bouquets of flowers on the floor.

"First off," said Carla. "What's the deal with all this stuff?"

"They're all from Victor. He's trying to…." She rubbed the back of her neck with her hand. "I found out something yesterday that changes everything."

Carla's eyes opened wide. "Really? What?"

"At dinner, Victor's uncle announced he was pleased I had come under their dental umbrella."

"Excuse me?" Carla's eyes widened.

"That's what I said. It seems Victor led his uncle to believe I would sell to them. And he led me to believe he'd convinced his uncle not to keep pursuing the sale of my practice."

"Oh Remmie. So where does this leave you and Victor?"

Tears threatened to spill over the brim of Remmie's lower eyelids. "Nowhere. Just right where I was before. Except now, I feel like my heart is shattered."

Carla wrapped her arms around her best friend. "It will work out. You'll see."

Remmie pulled away and looked up at her. "Oh Carla, I appreciate that. But I'm wondering if you're just seeing everything through the eyes of someone newly in love."

"I, well, I suppose I am seeing only good things at the moment. But Remmie, I've seen you with him. Even when you were fighting. There was something there. You two have chemistry. It's obvious."

"I thought so too. But now…." She looked around at all the things that had been delivered just that morning. Flowers, candy, stuffed animals. She'd have to store most of it in her break room closet. Or, why not deposit it all in front of Victors' door? That way he'd get the message loud and clear and she wouldn't have to think of him every time she looked at it.

Darcy came in late, as usual. "Oooh. Stuffed animals. Can I have one?"

"No," said Remmie, "you can't have one. I'm not keeping them."

With Carla and Darcy's help, Remmie lugged everything outside. It took several trips. Remmie didn't even want to know how much it all cost. But then, Victor had plenty of money. He and his uncle made sure of that.

Two patients walked up to Victor's door and stepped around the stacks of stuff. It didn't block the door. That wouldn't be fair to the patients, but they'd stacked it in front of Victor's large front window. He'd see it soon enough. Or one of his patients would make a comment about it.

Remmie glanced into his front window. She quickly turned away. What was she doing? Hoping for a glimpse of Victor? No. She wouldn't stand there and gawk at his office, willing him to come out. Where would that get her? Somehow, she had to get over him. Stop thinking about him. Even though he was right next-door. *Good luck with that, Remmie.* She forced her feet back to her own office.

A half hour later, Remmie's front door opened. Expecting her next patient, she pulled the dental chart out of her stack of patients for the day. The man who entered definitely wasn't Mrs. Gibbons.

"What do you want, Victor?" Remmie stared at him. Standing there in her lobby. Piercing her with his blue eyes.

"Remmie, why did you return all the gifts?"

"Because I want nothing to do with you. Didn't you get that message last night? Or are you just dense?" She put her hands on her hips.

He frowned. "I was hoping—"

"What, that the gifts would win me over? That I'd forget about all you've put me through? I don't think so."

Victor looked down at the floor. "I'm so sorry, Remmie. I tried to tell my uncle, over and over, that you weren't interested in selling. He wouldn't hear of it. He's convinced that the proximity of our offices is too good an opportunity to pass up. He kept pushing."

"But the other part of that equation, Victor, is that I don't want to sell! I'm just…honestly how many times do I have to say it? Yet you kept pushing me."

Victor took a few steps toward Remmie. Carla made herself scare and darted into the back of the patient area, dragging Darcy along with her. Remmie narrowed her eyes at Victor.

"What are you doing?" She took a step back.

He frowned. "Nothing. What do you mean?"

"Whenever you get closer to me, you're coming in for a kiss."

He smiled. "Would that be so bad?"

"Yes." She crossed her arms. "It would be the worst thing in the world right now."

"Remmie, you've wounded me." He smiled again.

"Cut it out Victor. I'm not going to let you kiss me, and your teasing and jokes don't cut it anymore. I'm over you. I think you should leave. Don't you have a patient waiting?"

Victor sighed. "Yes, I have someone waiting. I just thought—"

"Well, you thought wrong." Remmie turned and marched back toward her patient area. She didn't even look behind her to see if Victor was still there. She didn't peek her head around the corner to check until she heard the front door open and close. Then she looked.

He was gone.

****

That evening, Remmie sat on her couch with Winston and Charles. She smiled at them. They always seemed to know when she was feeling down. How did they do that? How did they know she needed them both beside her, snuggled close? Giving her extra purrs and nose kisses?

"Well guys, it looks like it's just us again. Although we weren't with Victor all that long before it fell apart, were we?"

Charles rubbed her hand with his face. Winston purred even louder.

She ruffled Charles' fluffy forehead. She adored her cats. They were her babies. And she got great satisfaction from her work. But, wasn't there more to life? Didn't she deserve happiness? Love? She'd thought Victor was it for her. She was wrong. So wrong. Sure, at first she was attracted to him, but couldn't see them together. But then, it seemed he had changed. She let down her guard. Let him into her heart. And just look where that got her. More alone than before.

****

Victor finished his patient. He filled out the patient chart after removing his gloves, mask and safety glasses. As his assistants cleaned up the room and prepared another chair for his 10:00 root canal, he headed to his office. He sat in his office with the door closed. He rested his head in his hands, elbows on the desk. What had he done? He couldn't blame Remmie. He'd be mad and hurt, too, if this had happened to him. Tobias' latest call early this morning wasn't pleasant. But when were they ever pleasant? He thought back to his teen years, trying to please his uncle. He never seemed to measure up. No matter how hard he worked at it. But wasn't that how Remmie was feeling? Wasn't he doing the same thing to her? He massaged his temples, trying to ward off a headache.

He raised his head and leaned back in his chair. There had to be a way for him to make it up to Remmie. Kind of difficult though when she'd barely speak to him, and returned his flowers, candy and stuffed animals. Looking at the situation now, he could see he went about it all wrong. Remmie wasn't the kind of person to be bought off. Not with her practice, and certainly not with those gifts. That wasn't her at all. That was what Victor had grown up with. Being rewarded with material things. Only if you did something right. But where did that get you? Alone. Frustrated. Heartbroken.

****

Remmie bolted through the front door, waving a newspaper "Carla. You have to see this."

Carla hurried through the doorway from the back of the office. "What?"

Remmie held out the newspaper. "Check out the ad on the back of the paper."

Carla frowned as she read it. "So, Victor has an ad for his office. Okay…"

"No, look at the very bottom."

Carla skimmed the words some more. "Oh, wow. What a typo. Wonder who will get in trouble for that?"

"I don't know. But how could someone make a mistake like that? People will come here to collect those great gifts Victor ordered. And I won't have anything to give them."

Carla handed the paper back. Remmie looked at it again. "What am I supposed to do?" The ad was full page, color, and eye-catching. Pictures of the same items she'd seen in Victors' delivered box were displayed there. Had Victor done this out of spite? Because she wouldn't sell to him and wouldn't see him anymore?

She picked up the phone and dialed Victor's cell phone. She had to leave a message. "I'm not sure what's going on with this ad in the paper, Victor. But we need to get this straightened out. Meet me at the Burger Barn tonight at 6:00. I'll expect to see you there."

Remmie didn't care if it was convenient for Victor or not. She needed to see him. Not for enjoyable reasons, either. That's why she didn't want him to come to her house. Even as mad as she was, he had a way of making her lose all sense of reason when they were alone. She thought back to the grocery store parking lot and outside her office the first night they went out. Hmmm. So sometimes even when they weren't alone. Hopefully there would be enough people in the restaurant that she could say what she needed to and be on her way. With no lip action involved.

****

The Burger Barn, one of Remmie's favorite places on earth, was crowded. Good. The more people the better to keep Victor from trying to kiss her. She'd make him keep his distance. She ordered a diet soda and fries and sat at her table. People all around her were laughing, smiling, and having fun with family or friends. Tonight wouldn't be a happy experience for her. She'd give anything not to have to see him again. But she also couldn't have patients showing up in her office expecting free gifts she didn't have. She'd look like a fool. Sipping from the straw of her diet coke, she kept an eye on the front of the dining room.

She spotted him at the order counter. He turned toward the dining area with his tray of food. Strange, seeing him with a burger and fries. Even though he met her here tonight, she hadn't expected him to actually eat. He seemed much more comfortable in upper scale restaurants. Like Fond Memories. That brought back a whole crop of memories on its own. She stuck up her hand, letting him know where she was. May as well get it over with.

Victor smiled as he skirted around tables of families. He had to step over two toddlers who were playing with toys on the floor. Even more than the food he carried, it was odd to see him smile around little kids. Although that day at the school he seemed okay with them. She didn't know what to think. Who was Victor, really?

"Remmie, I'm so glad you called me."

As soon as he'd sat down and placed his food on the table, she leaned forward.

"Don't think this is you and me getting back together."

His smile fled. He blinked. "Um, right. Your message said you wanted to talk about the newspaper ad."

"Yes. First of all, was it a giant typo on the paper's part? Did some dunce down there get our offices mixed up since we are right next door?"

Victor took a bite of his sandwich. Remmie waited for him to grimace, growl or choke.

He tilted his head. "Hmmm. Not as bad as I expected. Wouldn't necessarily feed it to the pigs." He smiled.

"Victor get serious. I asked you a question."

He set down his sandwich. "No, Remmie, it wasn't a typo."

He *admitted* it. "So you put the ad in there just for spite?"

He shook his head. "No, of course not. Why would you think that?"

She huffed out a breath and leaned closer. "What am I supposed to do when people show up expecting watches and jewelry?"

"You smile and hand it to them."

Remmie frowned. "What's wrong with you?"

"Besides being a snake or a you-you?"

She was getting steamed now. She wanted to yell at him, but couldn't with all the people around. Maybe that part of her plan backfired. She whispered, "How am I supposed to do that when I don't have anything to give them?"

"The box of gifts will be in your office."

She squinted. "Come again?"

"You'll have the gifts to give them. They'll be happy. You'll be happy. You'll have happy existing patients, and maybe get some new ones along the way."

She sat back. "Why are you doing this?"

"Because I'm trying to make it up to you."

She lowered her voice. "Victor, I can't afford to reimburse you for all that stuff."

"I don't expect you to. I never wanted you to."

"I don't understand."

He leaned toward her, holding her eyes with his stare. "Remmie, I want to do this for you."

"I don't believe you. You've got something up your sleeve. What's in it for you?"

He lowered his eyebrows. "Well, I can see it won't work out the way I'd hoped. But what's in it for me was supposed to be *you*."

He pushed his tray away from him on the table. Stood. And turned to walk away. Remmie's mouth hung open as she watched him leave the restaurant and head to his car.

****

He was trying to buy her. Again. Didn't he see that? Or did he think this was different than all the flowers he sent her the other day? Did he still think she would sell to him if he dangled enough chocolate in front of her? Remmie paced around her living room. Her cats watched her. Back and forth. Back and forth. It looked like they were watching a ping-pong match.

Remmie held up her hands. "What do I do, guys? Obviously I won't be accepting his offer to buy me out. That was never going to happen. And I could print a retraction in the paper about the gifts, but then I'd look like an idiot. And I'd have to pay for the retraction. I guess the best thing to do would be to hand out the gifts, then insist I pay Victor back over time. I don't want to be in his debt for anything. Not ever."

She looked at her audience. Two pair of green eyes stared at her, unblinking. Remmie smiled sadly. "You guys are such great listeners. Glad I have you. It's looking like you may be the only roommates I'll ever have. Not that I'm *not* crazy about you. You're my babies, after all. But, I thought Victor could be a part of our family someday, too." She sat down on the couch, pulling her babies close. Tears threatened to spill onto her cheeks. She would not cry. She would *not*.

****

Determined to make Victor listen to her, she marched into his office the next morning. His receptionist smiled. Her nametag said Candy.

"Hi, Dr. Grin. Are you here to see Dr. Barrett?"

Remmie smiled back. She wondered how the receptionist knew her. They'd never met before. "Yes, thanks. And, I'm sorry, have we met before?"

The young woman shook her head. "No, but Dr. Barrett talks about you all the time. In glowing terms. I'd know you anywhere."

Remmie frowned and tilted her head as the woman left to go get Victor. What was that about? Victor talked about her? In glowing terms? What exactly did that mean?

The man in question appeared. Gone was his usual smiley smirk. Gone were the jokes, the twinkle in his mischievous blue eyes. "Hi, Remmie. What can I do for you?" He pointed to the waiting area. Remmie preceded him to the chairs and sat down.

"Victor, I know what you said about me keeping the gifts. And I see no way around me handing them out, short of printing a retraction in the paper and looking like an idiot." She paused, giving him the opportunity to crack the joke she'd left open for him. Nothing. "So I've decided to accept them, but only if I can pay you back."

He held his hands out to his sides. "That's not what I wanted. That was never my intent. I was trying to help you out."

Was he serious? He wanted to help her instead of buy her practice? When had that changed? "I...I insist you let me pay you back." There. She'd said it. She crossed her arms and waited for his argument.

"If you feel strongly about it, then all right."

Where was the arguing, the joking, the flirting? She frowned. "Thank you."

"Is there anything else?" He pointed toward the back of his office. "I've got a busy day ahead."

"Uh, no. That was it."

"Okay, Dr. Grin. See you around. Maybe." He turned from her and headed back toward his patient area. Without a backward glance.

Dr. Grin? He used to never call her that even if she specifically asked him to. Something weird was going on. She just didn't understand what it was. And as strange as it seemed, she actually missed his obnoxious jokes and flirtation.

Chapter Thirteen

Remmie juggled her purse, pale pink scrubs on a padded hanger and a cardboard box full of toothbrushes that had come to her house instead of the office. Deciding there was no way she could dig through her purse while holding all the stuff, she set the box on the sidewalk with the clothes sitting on top. Where were those stupid keys? She needed something to help her locate them at times like this. Something like using the remote on her keys when she couldn't find her car in the parking lot. So, she needed a remote to find her remote? Now that just seemed silly. It sounded like something Victor would have teased her about.

"Oh, good morning, Dr. Grin."

Remmie turned around to see Tobias staring at her. "Good morning." Why did she have to run into him? The last time she saw him was in the restaurant with Victor. An evening she'd just as soon forget.

"I don't know how you did it," he said.

Huh? "Excuse me? Did what?"

"You finally got your way."

She frowned. Why was he being so belligerent? She didn't even know what he was talking about. She shook her head. "I know it's early and I haven't had my diet coke yet, Dr. Shultz, but what on earth are you talking about?"

"This." He reached into his briefcase and pulled out a stack of papers an inch thick.

"And that's supposed to mean...."

Tobias sighed. "Victor called me and said he no longer wants to do business with me. To be as he put it *under my thumb.* So these are papers he's going to sign to make it legal. He will no longer receive assistance from me in any form. He will have to pay me back a huge amount of money for dental school. To be blunt, Dr. Grin. He'll now be like you. Poor."

Tobias wrenched open Victor's office door, leaving Remmie alone on the sidewalk.

Remmie stood there with her hand still in her purse. The search for her keys forgotten. She couldn't move. Her mind couldn't process what Victor's uncle had just told her. Victor? Not doing business with his uncle? Poor? *Victor?*

She shook her head to clear it, located her pesky keys and opened the door. Dragging in the box and clothes, she shoved them behind her front counter and sat down at the desk. Flopping her purse on the counter, she just sat there. What on earth had happened?

Carla showed up four minutes later. She frowned. "What's up, Rem? Usually you're halfway through reviewing your morning charts by now."

Remmie looked up at her. "Carla, I ran into Victor's uncle outside."

"Okay. And…" She made the *continue* hand motion.

"He said…I can hardly believe this, he told me that Victor in essence split from him and doesn't want to do business with him anymore."

Carla set her purse on the counter. "But doesn't his uncle pay all the bills?"

"Yeah. Well, he did. Now I don't know what will happen. He even said Victor would be like me now."

Carla grinned. "Cute and sassy?"

Remmie gave her friend a weak smile. Then sobered. "No. Poor."

****

Remmie was all ready to run over to Victor's office. She had to find out exactly what happened. She opened her office door and stuck her head out. Just in time to see a family of four go in. Well, that wouldn't work. Victor would be busy for a while with them. Rats. Now she'd have to wait. She knew deep down it was none of her business. That she didn't have any right to ask. She had, in essence, split from Victor, too.

But... she couldn't stand not knowing. And it wasn't her usual cat-like curiosity, either. She opened the door wider and stepped outside. She wanted to talk to Victor, to see how he was doing. No matter what brought this about, he must be devastated. His uncle had been more than an uncle. He'd been a father figure. Such as it was. She shook her head. Now wasn't the time to see Victor, obviously. She'd just have to wait.

As soon as she went back inside, her first patient showed up. And he brought his seven-year-old daughter who had a toothache. And would Dr. Grin mind taking a look at her, also? Remmie sighed. She was going to be busy for a while, too.

Finally at lunch, she was free to check on Victor. She washed up after her last patient, helped Carla clean the room, and scooted out the door.

Going in to Victor's office, she smiled at his receptionist. "Hi, Candy, is Victor in?"

The young woman smiled. "No, I'm sorry. You just missed him."

Disappointment hit hard. "Oh, well, okay. Thanks."

"Should I tell him you were here?"

She shook her head. "No thanks. I'll try later." She needed to see him face to face. And she didn't want him knowing she'd been snooping around beforehand.

It was her turn to watch the phones, so she went back to the office. Carla was meeting Joe, and would bring her something to eat on her way back. She settled down at the desk with a diet soda and a cat magazine. She couldn't wait to see Victor. How was he? Was he upset? Why had he told his uncle he didn't want to do business with him anymore? It must have been something huge for Victor to do that. How many times had he told her he owed his uncle and needed to work for him? She couldn't imagine him doing what he did lightly.

Her afternoon morphed into a nightmare of patient problems. Her root canal didn't go well and took an hour longer than expected. Her extraction patient was frightened and had to be calmed down before they could even start. And her last patient, who needed four fillings, showed up twenty minutes late. Besides that, she'd run out of her favorite restorative material and had to settle for something that took longer to manipulate into the desired results. She thought she'd never get done.

At the end of the workday, Remmie was determined to see him. Carla assured her she and Darcy could handle the clean-up by themselves, and insisted Remmie go see Victor. She dashed out the door and trotted over to his front entrance.

This time, she got lucky. The receptionist looked up. "Hi, Dr. Grin. He's just about done if you'd like to wait a few minutes."

Remmie smiled. Would she ever? She sat down in one of the waiting room chairs but was too fidgety to sit still. She paced around the small area rug. Back and forth. Back and forth. She giggled, remembering doing that in front of her cats in her own living room. She heard footsteps and looked up. Nope. Just the receptionist and assistant leaving for the day. She smiled and waved as they made their way out the door.

She sighed. What would she say to him? Should she blurt out what Tobias told her? Should she make small talk and wait for him to bring it up? Neither seemed right. What she ended up saying was a little different.

Victor came out into the waiting room area. His steps halted. "Remmie? What are you doing here?"

Now what? What should she do? Only one thing came to mind. "Is it true, Victor?"

He stared at her. "You know, don't you?"

"Yes, I ran into your uncle this morning."

Silence.

She took a step closer. "Is it true?"

"Yes."

"Why?"

His blue eyes bore into hers. "You really want to know?"

"Yes. For Pete's sake just tell me." She tapped her left foot on the carpet.

Victor rubbed the back of his neck with his hand. "I told him I wasn't going to pressure you any more about selling. And he said he guessed I would have to pay him back for dental school. I know him, Remmie. He was using that as a bluff to coerce me into pressuring you again."

"Okay…"

"I called his bluff."

Remmie gasped. "You did this for me?"

"Yes. You're the only reason I would ever do it."

Remmie didn't even remember moving. She ran toward Victor and jumped in his arms before she realized it. She threw her arms around his neck. Kissed his cheek. His lips. Again and again.

Victor raised his eyebrows. "Not that I'm complaining, but what brought this on?"

"Now I know you weren't lying before."

"No, I wasn't lying. But it took this for you to believe that?"

She lowered to the floor, but didn't let go of him. "Victor, it's all been very confusing for me. The pressuring me to sell, the constant bickering, and leading me to believe you'd fixed it all with Tobias."

He frowned. "I know. I'm so sorry, Remmie."

"And you tried to tell me that earlier. And I wouldn't listen."

He sighed. "But I don't blame you. You had every reason not to believe me."

"No, I'm sorry. I didn't believe you before, but when I found out what you did, splitting with your uncle. I just *knew*."

He took her hands in his. "So what happens now?"

She smiled. "I have a few ideas."

****

The mayor's face beamed as he welcomed half the city to outside the front of the office. The street was blocked off and people were crowded around. Newspaper reporters snapped pictures and held microphones. Carla and Joe stood off to the side, smiling at Remmie and Victor. The four of them had gotten very close in the last few months, spending so much time together getting things ready for today. Darcy stood off to the side, flirting with a reporter.

Victor put his arm around Remmie's shoulders. She leaned into him, inhaling his spicy aftershave. She looked up at him. He leaned down for a quick kiss. She smiled, remembering how they'd first met. How she didn't think it could ever work out between them. Now, she couldn't imagine a life without Victor. Looking down at her hand, the diamond and garnet engagement ring sparkled in the late fall sunshine.

The mayor grabbed a microphone, although with his booming voice, didn't really need one. "Welcome, everyone! I'm so pleased to be a part of this special celebration. If my wife will hand me the two pairs of scissors, we'll get this ribbon-cutting underway."

Victor and Remmie were each handed a pair of scissors. Remmie glanced up at the new sign: Grin and Barrett Dentistry. She looked up at Victor and grinned.

"Ready for this, Dr. Barrett?"

He smiled back. "If you are, Dr. Grin."

"Just so you know, I'll have my section cut way before you do."

He laughed. "Wanna bet?"

The End

ABOUT THE AUTHOR

Ruth J. Hartman is a romance author as well as a licensed dental hygienist. She writes sweet, humorous romance novels. Often times they revolve around dentistry, cats, or both. She lives in rural Indiana with her husband of 29 years, and two extremely spoiled, fat cats.

Also by Ruth J. Hartman:
My Life in Mental Chains
Pillow Talk
Flossophy of Grace **Editor's Pick**
and
Purrfect Voyage

More about her books can be found at her website:
www.ruthjhartman.blogspot.com

If you enjoyed Ruth J. Hartman's *Grin & Barrett*
you might also enjoy these contemporary romance
authors published by Turquoise Morning Press:

Renee Vincent, author of *Silent Partner*

Maddie James, author of *Crazy for You*

Margaret Ethridge, author of *Contentment*

Thank you!

For purchasing this novel from
Turquoise Morning Press.

We invite you to visit our Web site to learn
more about our
quality Trade Paperback and eBook selections.

www.turquoisemorningpress.com

Turquoise Morning Press
Because every good beach deserves a book.
www.turquoisemorningpress.com

~~~~~

Sapphire Nights Books
Because sometimes the beach just isn't hot enough.
www.sapphirenightsbooks.com

Made in the USA
Charleston, SC
21 September 2011